In The Red Kitchen

Michèle Roberts was born in 1949, and is half French. She lives and works in London. Her previous novels are *A Piece of the Night*, *The Visitation*, *The Wild Girl* and *The Book of Mrs Noah*. She is co-author of four books of poetry. Her two solo poetry collections are *The Mirror of the Mother* and *Psyche and the Hurricane*. She has also written short stories and essays, and her play *The Journeywoman* was premiered in Colchester in 1988.

*Also by Michèle Roberts and
available in Minerva*

The Wild Girl

MICHÈLE ROBERTS

In The Red Kitchen

Minerva

A Minerva Paperback
IN THE RED KITCHEN

First published in Great Britain 1990
by Methuen London
This Minerva edition published 1991
by Mandarin Paperbacks
Michelin House, 81 Fulham Road, London SW3 6RB

Minerva is an imprint of the Octopus Publishing Group,
a division of Reed International Books Limited

Copyright © Michèle Roberts 1990

A CIP catalogue record for this title
is available from the British Library
ISBN 0 7493 9115 4

Printed and bound in Great Britain
by Cox & Wyman Ltd, Reading, Berks

For Jim

Thanks to Ros Asquith, Sally Bradbery and Penny
Valentine for fun, food and support; thanks to Nicole
Ward Jouve for encouragement; thanks to Sarah Lefanu
and Caz Masel for reading and criticizing my final draft;
thanks to Alison Fell, Judith Kazantzis, Giuliana Schiavi
and Irving Weinman for writerly solidarity; thanks to
Marguerite Defriez for eating and shopping expeditions;
thanks to my parents for seeing me through; thanks to
Chandra Masoliver for moments of illumination; thanks
to Linda, Sam and Leo for their welcome and for letting
me re-imagine their kitchen; thanks to Caroline Dawnay,
my agent, and to Elsbeth Lindner, my editor at Methuen,
for their interest and support; thanks to Jim Latter for his
loving friendship.

Author's note

I have based one of the stories in this novel on the life of Florence Cook, the young medium at the heart of a nineteenth-century *cause célèbre*, but have freely adapted the (disputed) facts in the controversy for my own fictional ends. In the course of researching contemporary accounts of mediumship I came across an essay by Alex Owen on femininity and mediumship which proved invaluable in clarifying my ideas (in *Language, Gender and Childhood*, edited by Steedman and Walkerdine, Routledge & Kegan Paul, 1987). Another very helpful secondary source was Elaine Showalter's study of women and madness in nineteenth-century English culture (*The Female Malady*, Virago, 1987).

Flora Milk is a monster in silk skirts. She looks like a woman, but she's a devil underneath, the part you can't see. That's the truth, Mr Redburn, and you should know it. Someone's got to write and tell you, and it might as well be me. For a long time I've been closer to her than anybody, we were good friends once. But I've found out that she is corrupt. Evil. She sucks the life out of people, she pretends to love them, but she simply uses them, takes all they've got, then throws them away and moves on to her next victim. She doesn't *look* vicious, of course. Her trick is to charm you. Everyone falls for it at first. You did, sir, just a little, didn't you? Just like all the others.

She bewitches people. Then sooner or later they feel her teeth rip their throats, those red lips of hers stealing their lifeblood away. Don't think I'm exaggerating, because I'm not. I tell you, in earlier times she'd have been burnt at the stake. These days, she gets away with it. Most people don't see through her until it's too late, until she's robbed them of what they hold most dear. Like she has robbed me. I could have been a good medium, I know I could, but she wouldn't let me take my chance. There isn't room for another medium in Hackney. Only for her.

She is a liar, too, and a fake. She fools all those poor people who come to her for comfort for the loss of their loved ones. Collapsible rods to make spirit arms, trick slates with messages already written on them, rubber gloves to feel like spirit hands, slip-knots that undo in a trice, gauze coated with luminous paint screwed up small in her drawers then tossed out to make a ghostly cloud, all these things are easy enough to do once you've learned how from some other unscrupulous medium. She is up to every trick, and she has an accomplice for those she can't do on her own, when she is being closely watched. Most of her audiences are so in love with her, the ladies as much as the gentlemen, they forget to look sharp, anyway. All that I'm putting down on paper here is the truth, sir. I'll prove it to you. Listen.

*

The funeral carriage is badly sprung, despite the amount it cost to hire, and makes me feel sick. Black-gloved fist pressed to my teeth, I bite on the wad of black-edged handkerchief as we jolt forwards under the high entrance arch of the cemetery. Those tall black plumes on the hearse-driver's hat; won't he have to duck his head to get through? The hearse is ahead of us: I can't see it, don't want to. Rosina and Mother sit opposite me, both weeping. I don't weep. I've got to be the strong one today, get us through. My sweet father, shut up alone in the dark in his coffin. Like me when I was a naughty child, roaring and sobbing, and had to be shut in the kitchen cupboard to calm me down. Only after a long time did someone come and let me out, one of the neighbours I think it was, I don't remember. None of us can let Father out of *his* wooden cupboard. Soon, worms will struggle across his face, nibble his eyeballs, his nose. I taste salt: I *am* crying, despite all my efforts not to. And the painful cramp of indigestion deep down in my stomach, bile rising, desperate discreet burps into the big cotton handkerchief, white as Father's shroud.

I lean forwards to take Mother's arm and help her rise, the steps let down and our veils too, Rosina and I steering Mother up the steep gravel path in the obscene sunshine. The younger ones, where are they? I halt, look around. Yes, disgorged from the second carriage, Aunt Dolly circling them like a great black sheepdog. There's Uncle Bill and the cousins, and behind them a group of men with black armbands, must be Father's mates from the printing works. I duck my head to meet a sob halfway, then march on.

The grass edges of the main path are so neat. Closely clipped green, daisy heads ruthlessly lopped. Beyond them, stone angels hold back laurel bushes, speckled and glossy, a host of brawny saplings, but can't hush the rude clamour of blackbirds. The worms sing too, at their underground feast. The harsh black mesh of my veil stretches tightly across my mouth; like the soil over dead faces. A flash of red as a thrush pecks up a worm, one dart of the sharp beak and the bloodied broken body is tossed onto the bright green grass. Lips quivering, I press Mother's arm and steer her left into a narrow passageway lined with vaults, sealed stone doorways and blank stone windows, tightly packed like the houses in our street: why, the necropolis is just like home. Why haven't I noticed before? I've been here often enough for family funerals. Home is just like the cemetery; full of Mother's dead babies. Hush. Don't let Mother know I'm laughing behind my black curtain of crape. Hush. Don't think of *his* body stiff in the double bed and Mother's face red with crying laid on his chest. Think about cold things instead, about cold hard things, like who's going to pay for this ridiculous funeral, this gross extravagance? Mother burying her man will spare no expense; wait till the bill comes in and then see how she howls: Flora, Flora, whatever shall we do?

Ivy snakes everywhere, grasping strongly at stone crosses, hairy suckers reaching down through fissures in granite slabs to claw at the rotting bodies beneath. My boots are clotted with the rich compost of corpses. My nostrils are filled with the stench of those lilies in the vase beside Father's bed. A wreath of those same lilies, great throats trumpeting of death's victory, lies on the coffin being carried ahead, bumping up and down between four pairs of black hands. Careful with my dear one, oh careful. The lilies have eaten him, gulping his white flesh in their thick white mouths. We shall bury the lilies and they will spit him out into the mouths of worms.

Out of the grander main part of the cemetery now, down yet another side path. No stone houses here, no mausoleums guarded by lion-headed dogs, crouching half-naked women with claws and wings. A close-packed jumble of crosses and stone slabs, some half sunk in the earth, pulled down by lichens and moss. Halt. The graveside. Black lips of earth parted, ready to close over this new morsel. Having already swallowed two little sisters and a little brother of mine. I glance at three small white crosses. George, Kitty, May. Closed in the earth, but three wounds that must be re-opening in Mother's heart. And now the fourth, tumbled in to join them. Four of them asleep in their green cots. That's how we're supposed to think of it. He is not dead, he is merely sleeping, he has gone before us, he will rise again, his body will be glorious and new. Hold on to that promise. Let it support you as firmly as you support Mother on your arm.

Now the black-clad mourners surround the grave, the younger children standing next to me and Rosina, the little group of relatives and old friends straggling around the other three sides.

The pain inside me has shifted downwards, dragging cramps. I let go of Mother in order to clasp my belly. The sunlight distracts me. How carefully I shaded Father's eyes as he slept after the fit, his breath rattling through his slack swollen lips, spittle dribbling from his bloated purple tongue. I pulled down the thin blind; his nightgown; his eyelids.

Beside me Mother tenses. Wretch that I am to forget what she suffers yet cannot show. That good pride, her ballast. I squeeze her arm, look into her face. Her eyes don't meet mine; they are clamped on some distant point in front. Beyond the grave. I follow the direction of her gaze.

At first the sun dazzles me and I can't see. Then the green-gold mist fades from my eyes and I can focus on the row of black-clad figures opposite, on the white tombstones behind them, and on the woman standing on the cropped turf between the tombs, a silver staff in one of her hands, a tall jewelled crown rising above her black brows, a pleated white cloak falling from her shoulders. And, curved about her handsome haughty face, a curled white beard.

Then the earth drops away under me, opening up to let me in, the sky turning black in the pit of my stomach. I can't hang onto the air because it won't hold me up, only my elbows exist because someone is gripping them, but between them I'm nothing. I swing down into the dark.

Dearest Mamma, I write to thank you for your wise and affectionate letter, so full, as always, of comfort and good advice. How good of you to write so soon after your last. Don't fret yourself for me, sweetest Mamma – the only reason I did not reply by return was that this wretched indisposition makes me too weak to hold a pen. But yesterday Dr Felton came to see me, and today I am feeling much better. Nurse has settled me on the sofa by a good fire and fetched me my writing things, so that at last I may thank you for the Reverend Butler's little book. I keep it at my bedside, as you suggested, so that I may refresh myself hourly at its consoling source and thus fix my mind on the great truths of eternity.

As you say, we must be thankful that little Rosalie was spared any more suffering, and indeed I try to be, but oh, Mamma, it is very hard to bear the affliction of her loss. I know how much you wish me to be strong, and believe me, I do try most earnestly to get well as fast as possible, for I know how much William and the children need me to be restored to my old health and spirits and to take my place amongst them again. So for their sakes, and for yours, I endeavour to improve. All too often, I fear, I am seized with apprehension that little William and Henrietta will also be snatched from me, though God be thanked, they appear to be in the best of health. Charles and Harriet and Ralph have grown up so much during this sad time. They are an inexpressible comfort. More and more we notice how Ralph takes on a look of you. In front of them, of course, I try to be cheerful and serene, but when I am alone it is hard to feel resigned to my terrible loss. William says I must think of the future, and I do try, believe me. He is convinced that too much solitary *moping*, as he calls it in his dear brisk way, is bad for me, so he has given instructions for the children to receive their morning lessons here in my room, so that I may continue to supervise their education as before. How their high spirits exhaust me sometimes! But I am much stronger than I was.

William is so full of thought for my welfare. He is all that is most considerate. He has suggested, of his own accord, that he should sleep in the dressing room, for I fear my restlessness at night disturbs him, and you know how much he needs adequate repose, with such a heavy burden of work to bear at the laboratory. He has embarked upon some important new aspect of his research, but I do not know yet what it is. He does not like to discuss intellectual matters in what we playfully call *the sickroom*, for fear of over-stimulating my nerves. He speaks of sending me and the children to the seaside for a fortnight. That will set me up, I feel sure! How fortunate I am in my dear husband! His care for me is unceasing.

Yesterday, as I mentioned above, he brought his colleague Dr Felton in to see me (you will recall how dissatisfied we were with Dr Brack). Dr Felton says I may expect to be confined in November. At the moment the sickness is not so very bad. Dr Felton prescribed me a different tonic and assured William that sea air would be just the thing to complete my recovery. I had not liked to mention it myself, but Dr Felton seemed to understand perfectly what I needed. I told him he could not imagine how I yearned to be able to take up again my duties as a wife and mother, how patient William has been in tolerating my enfeebled state.

After the consultation Dr Felton had a word with William at the other end of the room, and this morning William moved his things into the dressing room and promised me that indeed I could go to the seaside after all. I feel the utmost tenderness for him! He complains only in the most loving and humorous way of all the extra burdens placed upon him by my illness, even when he is delayed at work and does not return home until ten o'clock, as has been happening increasingly of late, and I am unable to come downstairs to make tea for him. How fortunate I am to have such an understanding husband!

So you see, dearest Mamma, how well cared for I am, how liable, perhaps, to grow selfish and lazy, so wrapped about as I am with love and kindness! I hope there is no fear of that. I would not be your daughter if I did not retain a strong feeling of *my duty*. Here I must close, as my silly cough always seems to grow worse in the evenings, and tires me out.

Believe me, dearest Mamma, your most grateful and ever-loving daughter,

Minny.

My apartments in the summer palace are on the ground floor, opening onto a verandah and thence to the garden. The walls are painted with designs of lotus flowers, and waterfowl swimming between clumps of reeds. The floors are a mosaic of tiny tiles, blue and green and turquoise. The colours are cool and restful; they help to keep the scorching heat at bay. The proportions and decoration of my rooms are symmetrical, perfect. Everything here has been chosen by me, and nothing may be moved or touched without my permission. I constantly rearrange the furniture, moving an alabaster jar to catch a shaft of late afternoon sunlight, draping the blue linen curtain at the doorway into more graceful folds, ensuring the ebony and ivory bedstead is in exact alignment with the angle of the wall. Any servant foolish enough to do more than dust and sweep is whipped then dismissed. My hands alone may touch my low table of cedarwood, my chests and boxes banded in gold. My hands alone may compose my kingdom.

This little world is all mine. It encloses, expresses and reflects me. It is beautiful and perfect. It is the place where I receive the King.

I sit behind the low balustrade of pierced white stone, contemplating the square of vivid green turf beside the oblong blue pool over which dart shimmering-winged insects and birds, the shadows flickering on the white gravel path that turn it pale lavender. Now and then a dry leaf falls with a rustle, a click, from the fig tree. Next to it, the huge date palm rears its droop of torn green across the stretch of grass, uniting it with the palace so that the outside becomes another room, its ceiling dappled by green shadow, its flowerbeds screened by the long slit fans of the palm.

My garden is a jewel flung down in brown sand. My garden is a square patch of green reclaimed from the desert, its brightness hemmed by brownish-yellow sand stretching away on every side until it dissolves into the sky. Egypt: a great long brown canvas with a narrow strip worked down its centre in vibrant blue and green silks. At its cultivated heart, my warm perfumed garden, irrigated by a canal dug through from the Nile. In times of drought the servants carry the canal here on their backs in stone jars, to water the creepers, the flowerbeds, the grass. My garden must not fail.

I lie on a heap of cushions; jade, sour yellow, lime. A light breeze strikes me with the scent of lilies, thick white blossoms in an alabaster pot inlaid with porphyry. I am waiting for the sunset, for the round red sun to dive behind the palm trees and suffuse the sky with pale pink light, a soft explosion like the inside of a giant shell; pearly, an intense blush, rosy, pushing across. I am waiting for the King to come to me.

A lizard pulses his red throat. A rasping sound from behind the hedge: the gardener brushing up fallen leaves and petals with his twig broom.

Pleats of the finest white linen fall away from me. My collar and bracelets are of gold set with turquoise, my sandals of plaited leather are fastened with gold cords, the belt tightly wrapping my waist is sewn with turquoise beads. My women have washed and anointed my body, oiled my hair then polished it with linen cloths until it shines like a black sun. I am ready.

The King will come to me by way of the garden, walking lightly along the colonnade of stone palms by the blue pool, his attendants holding up the fringed canopy above his head.

I am Hat, sole daughter of the Pharaoh, sole princess of the blood royal of the Two Kingdoms of Egypt.

My father is the King and he will come to me.

The walls of this house are built of grey brick. When I look more closely I see they are not grey at all but blue, dark yellow, burnt brown, plum. The window frames and ledges, painted cream a long time ago, are peeling and flaking now. The front porch, with its twin columns of chipped stucco, frames a door in faded olive green that grips two tall oblongs of stained glass. The wrought-iron bootscraper is blurred with dirty white paint. A patch of earth between the house and the street, no railings or fence, is choked with rubbish. But a thin plane tree still straggles up outside the tall ground floor window, braving the dust and traffic fumes, and a bush of Michaelmas daisies, a clump of snapdragons, orange and yellow and dusky pink, still hang on at its foot.

From the back room a French window, pearly and opaque, edged with strips of apricot and dark blue glass, leads into an overgrown garden, brambles coiling above old bedsteads and bits of broken bottle, a few late roses bright against dandelions and chickweed, sycamore saplings seeded in the wild grass under the blackened brick wall at the far end. I come out into the back garden to perch on a splintery wooden box and drink cups of tea in the intervals of work. I like this tunnel of back gardens, choked with greenery, enclosed and hidden by streets. The individual houses, tall and thin, make our lives vertical; but in the back-to-back gardens we can spread out sideways, sprawl through fuchsia bushes, pollarded plane trees, beds hot with marigolds and dahlias. But the garden will have to wait. First I must attend to the inside of the house.

I've never owned property before now. Could never afford it. I was left at my aunt's house in a wicker basket decorated with straw roses that fitted tightly round me. I was wrapped in a scarlet woollen blanket, I wore a striped helmet with earflaps, pink and green, and there was a big comb tucked in with me, black plastic with bits of diamanté. My aunt told me when I was older that she threw these items away, unsuitable.

From my aunt's house I was despatched to the convent, aged seven. I grew up in brown serge gymslips, thick beige stockings, brown capes. The statues in the school chapel wore exotic clothes: the Holy Infant of Prague preened in green velvet threaded with silver, lace ruffles, a purple silk stole, and the Virgin was decked in pale blue satin with a pearl-embroidered white cloak and gold roses on her toes. The chaplain tottered in stiff splendid frocks sewn by the black-garbed sacristan and her team of short-sighted novices: green brocade in Advent, purple and violet in Lent, gold and white at Easter. The nuns' dark habits were a wool-polyester mix, washable; their nightgowns were good old-fashioned flannel, inherited from sisters dead twenty years before. Later, the Order updated itself; the starched, winged head-dresses and full black skirts, the dress of Norman peasant women worn by the Foundress as a girl in Rouen, were exchanged for short ugly overalls and skimpy grey veils.

When I left the convent school at sixteen, I clothed myself from jumble sales. For fifty pence I bought a tea-gown in black crêpe-de-Chine, the sleeves, full to the tight wrist, flowered in a crazy garden of colours, the body and skirt cut on the bias, darted and seamed to hug then flow in a mermaid's tail about my ankles. I fought another woman for it; I won. I wore it most days; in cold weather I topped it with a quilted scarlet thirties dressing-gown. I wore it with a pair of boots I painted gold, a scarlet patent-leather belt, a black felt sombrero, and earrings that dangled green feathers. My ideas of style came from the statues in the chapel, and from the priest's vestments. I've never been interested in formal good taste in clothes. Elegant restraint depresses me: it reminds me of the nuns' habits, and the pupils' gymslips.

My first employer bought me more fancy dress: a chauffeur's uniform. I insisted she add a cap with gold braid. She was an Old Girl of the convent, whom I met at a reunion tea the summer after I left. Over dry sherry and macaroons in the parlour we sized each other up. That day she wore jodhpurs and riding boots; having lost her licence because of dangerous driving, she had arrived on horseback. She was a widow of eighty, still beautiful. She said she wanted to make up for lost time. I drove her around northern France that July and August. Sister Julian taught me to drive, first on the tractor down on the nuns' farm in Sussex, then in what was referred to as our Morris. Sister sat in the back, saying the rosary while I cavorted across roundabouts.

The long straight roads in Normandy were spattered with sun slicing through the limes and poplars; I found myself applying prayer as I applied the accelerator, the rhythm of Hail Marys opening me up to full throttle. Mrs Armstrong, like Sister Julian, sat in the back, our picnic lunch in a hamper on the seat beside her. She approved of my driving, she approved of my quickly-acquired relish for French food, she approved of my gold boots which I wore with the chauffeur's uniform. I felt at home in France; the language sang to me and I sang back to it. We stopped at various convents of the Order, to relay gifts and messages from the exiled nuns in England; we slept between linen sheets in high narrow beds in spotless airy guest rooms; we were served a variety of homemade herbal liqueurs. In Rouen we were shown the incorrupt body of the Foundress hidden under the altar in the chapel; the priest might not touch it, though he said Mass over it every day.

At the abbey in Fécamp, I was left to sightsee while Mrs Armstrong sipped Bénédictine with the bishop before lunch. Outside, the paved streets were grey with rain. Inside, the stone was scoured to creamy yellow, the black rows of straw-seated chairs and uncomfortable prie-dieux dwindled to matchboxes under the soaring roof. There was nothing to distract from prayer, no pious plaster statues or stiff bouquets, just this wide open embracingess, an enclosed space that was empty yet full as an egg. My footsteps fell into the silence. The vaulted aisles tugged at my shoulder-blades like wings, the serene complications of leafy capitals sprouted inside me, the columns leapt like my legs could. Then my eyes, dragged upwards to the high air propping the roof, understood my fragility, how this great church's balance could rock, tip, crush me. My knees shook; I wanted to flee. Rain drummed outside. I hid in an empty confessional of carved black oak, pulling the little purple curtain behind me to shut out the draughts. I had entered the wrong side: the priest's. There was his breviary, his purple stole hung on a hook, his newspaper folded open at the sports page. I stayed where I was, liking the smell of holy dust, aftershave, incense. I fingered an ashtray on the ledge in front of me, the squashed stub of a Gitane. A rosary coiled next to it, little carved wooden beads like juniper berries, peppercorns.

The voice came from the other side of the grille, the little cubicle where the penitent kneels in the darkness. It was a woman's voice, low and clear.

Filet de boeuf en croûte, it said: *marrons glacés, haricots à la crème, tarte aux pommes des demoiselles Tatin.*

The rosary beads tilted through my startled fingers. It wasn't Mrs Armstrong's voice I was hearing: she spoke French with a pronounced English accent. And the church had seemed empty.

The voice came again.

Gâteau de Savoie. Coquilles St Jacques. Maquereaux à la façon de Quimper. Tripes à la mode de Caen. Moules Marinières.

I jumped out of the confessional, ran round to the other side, pulled open the curtain and peered inside. No one there.

The nuns would have said that a voice you hear in an empty church is either that of God or that of the Devil.

It was neither of these. It was a third voice. Briefly imprinted on the glossy black oak of the cupboard-like, oven-like confessional, I saw a cavernous underground kitchen, lit by the red glare of flames, a giantess in sabots stoking her fire then setting a great black frying pan on it; the swirl of a yellow omelette, the hiss of butter.

– Hattie! Hattie!

This time it was Mrs Armstrong calling. I walked to meet her, knowing that my vocation had been announced to me.

Soon after our return to England, my good employer and benefactress died of a stroke. She left me an excellent reference, and a month's salary in advance, just enough to live on while I looked for my next job. I cooked for another Old Girl; the convent looked after its own. At night, sitting up in bed, I wrote my first book.

Sister Bridget at the convent, during my shifts as food monitor in the kitchen, had described to me, with much sighing and clicking of teeth, the secret of soda bread and scones, how to stew good plain dishes from cheap cuts of meat using cloves and onions and a dash of Guinness, how to make jams and preserve fruit and vegetables. This was all reminiscence; the nuns, like the pupils, ate bones and gristle and fat, sour greens, soapy carrots. She taught me that to cook well you have to love the ingredients themselves, and the people you are cooking for. She said this was difficult in the convent. It was her cross.

As we mashed green-eyed potatoes and peeled swedes and

turnips we said the Office together, the words of that poetry working themselves into the foodstuffs between our fingers like sweet and bitter herbs. When the bell rang for the Angelus, late morning and late afternoon, we stood in front of the little bracket bearing a statue of the Virgin, and saluted her: Christ leapt in her womb as the bread leapt in the oven, Christ burst from the tomb as the parsnips boiled over. Yellow food in that kitchen. Yellow root vegetables, yellow chips, yellow steamed pudding pitted with bits of black date, yellow custard.

Also I wrote down the recipes that the nuns in France, when I wheedled, had given to me. Their kitchens had blue and brown tiled floors, brass and copper pans hung in racks above the stove, tall blue china jars of coffee and chicory. In those days the nuns were divided along class lines: choir sisters, lay sisters. The choir sisters, who did no physical work, always said how holy the lay sisters were as they scrubbed and washed. Sœur Marie-Madeleine of the motherhouse in Rouen taught me words in Norman patois while she showed me how to make the little boat-shaped cakes named after her patroness, how to make nuns' custard tarts flavoured with almonds on a base of apricot jam, how to cook kidneys in red wine, brains in butter, liver in Calvados with apples and cream.

I called my cookery book *Leaves from a Convent Kitchen Garden*. Hitting just the right note of nostalgic chic, it sold well enough to finance a second trip to France, this time on my own. I walked all over Burgundy, reading Colette as I went, the pages impregnated with the scents of mushrooms, truffles and chestnuts. Mists wound along the river valleys and through the walnut orchards. Scarlet vine leaves lined the baskets on which the women laid out their cheeses to sell at market. I wrote another book of recipes, this time imagining the meals Colette greedily tucked into with Sido, with Missy, with the music hall artistes, with the modernist lesbians at Natalie Barney's salon. *Eating Me Eating You*, published by a feminist house, did not do quite so well as its predecessor (Colette has never had her due from the English) but I was content. I was following out my vocation.

I found work as a freelance part-time cook for small restaurants, cafés, wine-bars. I earned just enough to live on. Our postage stamp, our Wellington boot, our soup plate, the nuns used to say. I didn't go to those lengths, but I enjoyed remaining rootless for over ten years, drifting between other people's homes, sometimes staying in a woman friend's flat, sometimes renting a room from acquaintances or living in digs, camping out on friends' sofas when times were hard. I fixed up each place I lived in, for however short a time; I had the knack of making the dingiest rooms beautiful; but evictions, my friends' changes in fortune, my own restlessness, meant that I always moved on, with my collection of cookery books, my pictures, my little wicker armchair, my plants, my collection of old cookery utensils, my bits of old china.

As I grew older, moved into my thirties, I began to want a home of my own. I reminded myself I had no money: another cookery book had not noticeably increased my wealth; publishers appeared to need money more than authors did. *Recipes for Death*, initially inspired by the Tutankhamun exhibition catalogue with its descriptions of the meals left in tombs for the spirits to enjoy, brought me some small fame, a few hundred a year in royalties. I continued to spend my Saturdays in street markets, acquiring worn bits of linen and lace, two threadbare but still beautiful kelims, the odd ladle, the odd pretty plate. In dreams I returned to the tiny flat I once squatted, only to find it much larger than I remembered it, corridors opening off to disclose room after room, delight as new spaces unfolded in front of me, a little maze of parlours, a nest of secret places.

I shut my dream away but kept it intact: a self-contained flat in an old building, high up and airy, with all my things in it; a home I couldn't be thrown out of, that would not dissolve, a centre that held me safely, that told me I belonged, that rooted me in warmth, that would let me grow at my own speed. As a gesture towards realizing my dream I taught a cookery class two nights a week, putting my earnings straight into the building society; my savings were small, but I liked the work, the women who came to me wanting to learn, the ribald stories we told each other as we beat and whipped and chopped. We wrote a cookery book together, mixing stories and recipes; it had a modest success, and I was newly content, even though the cookery class was disbanded shortly afterwards because of the cuts.

I bought this house just before the last boom in prices. It was reasonably cheap because it was, is, a wreck, and miles from the nearest tube. There is little housing now in London affordable by the homeless poor. Least of all is there housing for the single poor. The number of homeless people in London, I read in the newspaper recently, has doubled in the last ten years. I found myself a home just in time. A barricade against the destitution and despair I see daily on the street, into which I could so easily have slipped. The people sleeping out in cardboard boxes under the railway bridge across from the shops; the young people begging outside the supermarket; the women hung about with children and pushchairs who beg at the bus stop opposite; the old man with all his possessions in a wire supermarket trolley which he pushes up and down the road; the old woman who sleeps in the entrance to the chemist; the man who wears a sack and a plastic carrier bag on his head like a chef's hat. I could so easily have been one of them. It always astonishes me when I meet people who own a house or flat; or when I read novels about people who do. They seem, so many of them, to take it for granted: normal, ordinary. To me it's a miracle I own this house.

Not a miracle. Hard work. I went on the game to raise the money for the deposit. I couldn't think of any other way to do it. I didn't admit to myself what I was up to, chatting up an acquaintance in the pub and then letting him do it to me for money in his car. I slipped into it easily, like several other women I knew at that time who drifted in and out of prostitution depending on the state of their finances; it was what you did for a while when your man deserted you and the children, or your benefit was stopped for some reason, or your heating was about to be cut off. I didn't call it prostitution. I simply charged men for sex. The nun inside me was scandalized at what she called my lack of self-respect. The policewoman inside me cautioned me against rape, getting into the clutches of a pimp, getting a record. But I discovered I was a good actress: I could be the degraded angel, the ever-welcoming mother, the tart with the heart of gold, the severe nanny, whatever the men required. I knew how to please. I stopped after a year, because I wasn't making enough money. I lived for three months on what I'd managed to save, and hastily wrote another book of recipes. *Gourmet Sex*, written under a pseudonym, was a minor bestseller, a how-to book for armchair foodies and sexual snobs. It was an exploitative book all right, full of lies. But once I'd sold the rights to America I had the money for the deposit on the house. Paying the mortgage isn't easy, since I've gone back to part-time cooking at the Hannibal Dining Rooms down the road, to leave me time to research and write my next book, but I don't mind. I've got what I always wanted, and I've kept my independence as well.

I met you by accident. I had no wish to fall in love; I'd overdosed on men; I felt I was a widow, and wore my weeds with aplomb. How could you have known I was a widow? Black was the fashionable colour last spring; all the women in my neighbourhood were wearing it. Celibacy suited me as well as my new black jeans. Men were a bad lot and always let you down.

Sheltering inside my tumbledown house I discovered that I was happy, that I enjoyed my life, that I was content to be single and alone. I went dancing with friends, I cooked and ate the meals I liked best, I devoured biographies of the great chefs, I sat up late devising recipes. Also I went for long walks by night, curving through the city and back and forth across the river. I smelt the river water, and beer, and creosote; sometimes I saw the silver moon sail high above cranes and building sites; I slid my hands along brick walls, sheets of corrugated iron, the sides of sweat-shops and factories. I re-connected myself to the city; I learned it again, after what had seemed my absence from it, by walking through it and touching it; I mapped its grimy heart and discovered how much I belonged in its dark windings. Under the bridges slept homeless people, soft shapes indistinguishable from sacks of refuse.

One night I found myself in a narrow alleyway in Wapping. Cobbles underfoot, tall black warehouses on either side, fences of old doors and barbed wire marking out a site of destruction, what's called development. Light melted from an open doorway. I went towards it.

Inside what I supposed was an old warehouse, the walls were invisible. I stood on cold stone flags; damp darkness coated my skin. An iron staircase next to me coiled upwards to a source of bright light, a din of chatter. A sense of vaults above me: I thought of the abbey church in Fécamp, also the underground stone kitchen awash with red shadows and red flames.

When you switched on the lights behind me I saw that the warehouse had been converted into a gallery. The brick walls were painted white and hung with large bright canvases that made my insides jump with pleasure, the floorspace was dotted with sculptures in bronze and iron. I could smell the river but not see it. I turned to look at you. Your red hair flew about your head.

Your bright blue eyes stared back at me. A big man, sturdy, with a bashed nose.

You'd come from the pub round the corner. You steered me upstairs, towards the party. This had been a friend's studio once, you told me, before rising rents had forced her out. You opened the warehouse doors onto the black drop of night and pointed down to the invisible Thames below. You fetched me food and drink and watched my enjoyment of everything you offered: stories, jokes, more wine. Everyone in the dense, very chic crowd at this show was in black, except for you in dark blue workman's shirt and battered cord trousers, and the artist, an auburn-haired beauty from New York in a low-cut evening frock of red brocade.

You offered me a lift home in your shabby little car. I trusted you, stupidly the nun inside me said, not to be a rapist; we swooped along the Embankment, past loops of pearl lights, shouting amicably at each other above the roar of your broken exhaust. Discovering we were both still hungry, we made a detour to a café in Waterloo for fried eggs on toast and cups of tea. You dropped me at my door and sped off. I fell into bed and dreamed I was the big woman in the warm red kitchen underground, beating out hoops of iron on an anvil to fix onto rows of wooden shoes.

Later you told me you first fell in love with me simply because of my appetite for wine and food and talk, my greedy liking of the world. My strong capacity for pleasure. You loved me for being exactly who I was. I told you about the things I'd done, the things that had happened to me, and you still loved me. You knew all about wheeling and dealing, the harshness of surviving in the city. You weren't surprised at what I'd got up to. I didn't want to fall in love; I wanted a pleasurable fling, no commitment, to stay in control. Your warmth breaks down my carefully built walls. Danger. Keep out.

It's evening as I sit and write this, high up in my house. Soft light from the lamp, the three candles I have stuck in saucers and placed about the shabby little sitting room. The uncurtained sash window is open, a black rectangle edged with frost; the glitter of purple; letting in cool air to mix with the breath of the fire around my neck, a scarf woven of different metals; hot, cold. Wasteful: a red fire burning while the window opens to the night wind tossing the invisible trees below; but I love it. A temporary union of opposites, the nearest I get to the idea of God, that makes me shiver inside with delight. I'm a whole, for a moment, enclosing heat and cold together; and I'm different parts, half belonging to heat and half to cold; I'm the point at which these two worlds meet.

In the warm and sombre light the dirty salmon of the wall above the fireplace is a pleasing colour. Little furniture yet: your battered wooden sofa with brown velvet cushions, dusty and squashy, that I lean on; my wicker armchair; my worn kelim, blue rose indigo; your little round table on high slender legs with arched scrolled feet; our joined record collection. My things mixed up with yours; new ingredients; a recipe for pleasure, for fear.

I've never kept a diary before. The past, my own past, has not mattered to me. Now, in this house, the past surrounds me and holds me, and my own past leaps back at me in flashes. Impossible to hold gleaming drops of water in my fingers; the past leaps away in a trail of silver; yet I need to go on trying to hold it, second by second. I want to tell you my stories. I want to record my life with you. I want to give myself a history. That's all.

I laze in front of the fire, bare feet up on the soft brush of the cushions made of red and purple bits of Turkey carpet, scribbling this. I'm bundled up in your old woollen dressing-gown, I'm lolling here in the half-dark in the tall thin shabby house, listening to the wind outside, a dog barking far away, a plane growling across the sky. A bunch of dark red tulips stands in front of the window; inside; reflected in a black mirror. Night presses up against them. The rain begins, silver pearls on black glass.

Sometimes, these nights of old age when sleep recedes to the corner of the bedroom and glares at me over one shoulder, a warm body refusing me, I still want to call out for Rosina, to pretend she'd come. Then I close my eyes just as I did in childhood and take the darkness inside, a whole soft black world in which colours fizz and spark like fireworks, melting and re-forming and melting again, the space behind my eyes a glowing loom weaving patterns I can swim in and out of as I watch. And my fingers pressed lightly to my closed lids can twist the glass of my kaleidoscope, cause stars to tumble, streams of blue to take new directions. So darkness becomes a homely place breathing in and out, an enormous room in which to fly free, roam unconstricted, turn somersaults.

Darkness has always been necessary to me. Now it is my one faithful companion. Waking at four a.m. as I so often do these days, I pull it around me as a comforter, and settle to continue writing this story of my life. For no reason except to please myself. There is no one else left to please except Lily, and she doesn't count. Jo returns to me sometimes in dreams, rising out of a pit of mud and fire, his brains hanging out of the hole scooped in his head, his bayonet clutched in his mittened fingers. I'm sleeping in the forest, he tells me: under a spread of leaves. William is dead too. I never saw him again after we came back from France, he wouldn't come and visit me. I heard he got the Nobel prize for science. You could say that was partly due to me. It makes no difference to this process of dying, which is hard work, which I do alone.

As a child in the dark I'm powerful. By day, less so, faced with the angle of the deal table jabbing my eye, those high hands going thump thump in the bowl of dough, those solid boots that shift to and fro and could crush my bare toes curling up from the cold floor. Backing away, I discover how the table recedes and grows smaller, a game I play trotting to and fro between the door and the broad aproned back, making the table grow big small, big small. Sometimes with a twist of raw pastry in my palm, for those hands slapping the dough into shape sometimes pause, that lap in the exhausted armchair can sometimes be safely climbed into. Power over those hands, that lap, that kissing mouth, it comes and goes, like the table.

Outside the house there are knees rushing towards me, and thick coarse jackets with bright buttons, and skirts that belly like clouds, like the washing on the line in our back yard. A red hand dives down from the sky of knees, encloses mine, pulls me along past fascinations I have no time to linger over and explore: brown coils of dog turds, jungle of yellow weeds behind rusty railings, perambulator wheels that squeak, the open hairy mouths of sacks, the great hooves of the dray horses. Dust flies in my face. Then the plop, plop, of warm rain, and a loud crack crack crack and the sky is blacked out by umbrellas going up one after the other, strong-winged birds.

At the dame school I learn my own name, as something apart from myself, as something I can create in front of me. Flora is a small slate framed by wood. I can be wiped clean with a wet sponge, then written in better. I know that's Flora there on the slate because the aniseed-breathing stout lady tells me so. I can leave myself on the slate and go outside to the privy, and Flora is still there when I come back. One day it all falls into place like dominoes lining up, click. One day I'm sitting in front of the book cupboard at the back of the classroom, looking at its doors pointed like churches, with purple curtains hung behind the glass, and wondering what it will be like to be able to read the books inside, and the next there's a book open on my lap, soft rag pages I can turn, black marks that mean something. I don't remember how this happened, how I've leapt from only knowing *table* because the lady has drawn a picture of it next to the white chalk mark on the slate into knowing *table* without the drawing. I can make *table* come and go on my slate, like the table in the kitchen in the house.

We practise writing, every day. *Book book book*, rows of *books* in copperplate. *Book* is small on my slate, big on my lap. The letters come alive: *h* is a thin man seen sideways seated on a chair, *m* is a man on all fours, *T* is my father, arms stretched out to greet me, *x* is when we do maze marching in the yard swinging our arms. But why is *h* used for *h*? Or *K* for *K*? I don't dare ask. Why not *p* or *r*? Who said?

My father packs letters into squares. Outside the house, at his job. I pass the high wall of the printing works on my way to school. His words are objects he holds in his hands. Made of metal, made by a machine. My father makes the pages of books, lifting letters one by one from the trays where they are kept in multiples like different sorts of sweets and arranging them into lines, backwards, like mirror-writing, in a frame called a forme. When he's filled it, he locks it into place so that no words fall out and spoil his neat sentences, then it's carted downstairs to the printing press.

My father recites to me the names of different typefaces, like poetry and hymns. Baskerville. Garamond. Bodoni. Bembo. He brings home broken bits of type for me to play with. He shows me how to fold sheets of paper into gatherings, stitch them together to make tiny books that he binds for me with scraps of cloth, a red thread as marker.

That's over. Long ago. I'm too busy helping Mother in the house, looking after the younger ones, to have time to play childish games like making books. I still read every one I can lay my hands on, though, stuffing myself with the tattered romances I pick up cheap on market stalls, collections of legends and fairy tales borrowed from the circulating library, working solidly through the family Bible; avid. Where do you get it from? Mother puzzles: much good will it do you. Put that foolishness down, will you. Come and help me. Down on my knees, mechanically brushing the stairs, still dreaming, the stories running through my head.

With Rosina I can act them out. Gone is the lethargy that descended after my father's death and lays me out so often on the sofa; gone, the headache that struck this morning; gone, the heaviness that makes me slow at household tasks and drives Mother into a worry I'm heading for an early grave; gone, the three younger children, to our neighbour's house; gone, Mother, to the chapel bazaar. Rosina and I have the whole house to ourselves.

Since I wrote to you last, my dear Mamma, I have had no fewer than three letters from you. You are much too good to your naughty child, spoiling her with so many affectionate remembrances and kind messages. Nor must I forget to thank you for the slippers. I am sure I do not deserve such thoughtfulness! Thank you a thousand times.

It was sweet of you, dearest Mamma, to offer to accompany me to the seaside in order to take the care of the children off my hands. But I could not have dreamed of burdening you, at your age, with my little monsters! In the event, our fortnight away passed off very well. Every morning Nurse took my darlings down to the sands so that I could be granted the rest and utter peace my soul craved after the grime and bustle of London. After a few days I found my health and spirits so improved that I was able to venture as far as the seat in the garden, and in a short while I was confident enough of my returning strength to begin to take short daily drives along the cliffs in the company of another lady from the boarding-house, a most agreeable person, and that of her brother.

Mr and Miss Andrews, I am sure you will be pleased to hear,

quickly became my intimate friends, their conversation proving their characters to be a most refreshing mixture of the elevating and the cheerful. Both were of most sympathetic temperaments, so that I quickly found that I could rely on their aid when any small difficulties with our life here arose. In the evenings, indeed, we formed quite a gay company, for Miss Andrews has a charming voice, and her brother plays the piano very well. On other occasions we simply sat and talked. How grateful I was that dear William has always made a habit of reading to me from *The Times*: Mr Andrews is by occupation a journalist and I would not have wished to appear ill-informed! Thus the time passed away rapidly in the enjoyment of pastimes shared with these most congenial friends.

I must confess, I hardly ever saw the children! I rarely felt strong enough in the mornings to dress them myself or to supervise their games on the sands, and in any case Nurse was most anxious to prevent my becoming fatigued, and in the afternoons I could not help wishing to benefit from the agreeable advantages bestowed upon me by my acquaintance with the Andrews. Miss Andrews, who was of an unfortunately fragile constitution, could not always manage to walk further than her accustomed bench on the promenade, so that her brother very kindly pressed me to make use of his services as a companion and guide. Many a pleasant hour we spent sketching or botanizing or bird-watching, and I could feel myself growing, in that mild but invigorating climate, quite as rosy and robust as I was as a girl.

Now that I am back I do not feel quite so well of course, but that is only to be expected! It is so damp in Bayswater. If only we lived in Hampstead, like the Andrews do, I am sure my health would be much better. And the children are tiring, bless their hearts: their noise does rather disturb me. Still, I do not mean to complain, for that would be so selfish, given all William's generous care for my recovery.

William is very well. While we were away he was busy forming a new acquaintance whose usefulness to his researches into psychic phenomena will be incalculable. You remember that he recently finished his enquiries into the case of the famous Mr Home, whose authenticity as a medium he finally emphatically established? Since then he has not left off working indefatigably to ascertain how the methods of science may clarify and explain spiritualistic occurrences, which continue to be all the rage here in London, and certainly in Hampstead, according to the Andrews. The name of his new protégée is Miss Milk, though I began, almost immediately, to call her Flora – she is so young! Like a schoolgirl still (though she is all of sixteen) in her black dress and apron, and the sweetest yellow curls hanging down onto her shoulders. I dote on her already, although I have only known her a week.

I accompanied William when he called on her family. They live in a dreadful neighbourhood – Clarence Road, in Hackney. Have you ever been there? I assure you *I* have not! Little mean villas patched together with no proper entrances or front steps, a hall scarcely larger than a box, a parlour most unfortunately situated in the basement, next to the kitchen – the two tiny ground floor rooms, we were given to understand, are rented out to lodgers. Mrs Milk, in these circumstances, can hardly be called a lady, but she is genteel in her way, and her daughter is very charming indeed, and both seemed very sensible of William's condescension in visiting them.

Little Flora is, of course – but I daresay you have guessed already – a medium of apparently great promise. Her performances to date, or, as the cognoscenti say, *seances*, show her, William says, to be unusually well equipped as a sensitive, and already possessed of an astonishing mastery of the techniques, or perhaps I should simply say gifts, of clairvoyance and clairaudience. As well as demonstrating her powers at public meetings, she sits regularly with a private circle of friends, in her mother's kitchen. The spirits do not seem to mind the smells of boiled cabbage and boot blacking that our too-sensitive nostrils perceived! Indeed, it is a sobering, even a humbling thought, that the gift of mediumship should have been bestowed upon a young girl of such very modest origins and lacking in all education.

I confess I am quite wild to attend one of her seances. Oh Mamma, just suppose she were able to transmit some reassuring message from my darling little Rosalie! I have suggested to William that we should consider inviting her, and her mother of course, to hold a seance here; I feel sure the atmosphere in my drawing room, so spacious and quiet, will be conducive to Miss Flora's becoming entranced. The parlour we sat in at her mother's house was, frankly, repellently shabby, though adequately clean, and I would rather not have to return there in order to witness my Flora's powers. Here I must close, my dearest Mamma, for Nurse has been waiting to speak with me this past hour.

Ever your loving daughter,
Minny.

Very often the King sends for me to have breakfast with him. In the early morning, before the sun has climbed the sky, it is still cool. The light is pale and still, the palace is quiet, no one comes in to disturb us. This is one of my favourite times for being alone with my father. His spirit is still fresh from its travels during the night, and his mood is cheerful and calm. We eat little, for he disdains greediness as he disdains all carnal self-indulgence; warriors, he says, must be as keen and sharp as their spears, and my father is a great warrior, as well as being the wisest man in the land. Even a girl, he instructs me, can learn wisdom, if she is willing to put away the foolishness of her sex and submit herself to rigorous training; even a girl can learn to run fast, to hunt as well as a boy, to keep her body slender, supple and vigorous. I sit on a low stool next to his chair, and we drink milk together and eat bunches of grapes or handfuls of figs, and then he talks to me.

This morning he has a gift for me: a writing set exactly like that of the scribes; only made in finer materials as befits my loftier rank: a wooden palette, edged with ivory, holding cakes of red and black ink, a brush-holder and water pot of alabaster, a bunch of brushes cut from reeds, a linen bag of broken pieces of pottery and limestone for me to practise writing on. If I can show him that my skill has improved since our last lesson together, he promises, he will allow me to start working on papyrus. He watches critically as I suck the end of my reed brush to soften it, dip it in water and in ink, sweep delicate strokes onto the painted ostrakon in my lap.

Were I not a royal princess with my destiny already written on stone, were I the son of a potter or a baker or a mason, my best chance in life, he tells me, would be to enter a temple and learn to become a scribe. The barber, the weaver, the arrow-maker, the coppersmith, the furnace-maker, each one of these labours from

23

dawn till night, his body exhausted by his toil. The profession of the scribe is greater than any of these; it sets a boy on the path towards the gods. My father's scribes are learned men who know literature, mathematics, medicine, the secrets of religion. Copying and recopying the sacred texts during their long apprenticeship, they have become wise and are much respected. I, as a royal princess, owe it to my rank, my duty towards my father, to succeed no less well than they. So I dip my brush into the ink again and complete the hieroglyph with a steady hand.

To write is to enter the mysterious, powerful world of words, to partake of words' power, to make it work for me. To write is to deny the power of death, to triumph over it. To inscribe a person's name on the wall of his tomb, to describe his attributes thereupon, is to ensure that he will live forever. As the tomb cut into the rock is the doorway to eternal life, so the words painted on the false door of the tomb enable the spirit of the dead man to come and go as he pleases through the stone walls. Words mean life. The absence of words means death: being forgotten by men for all eternity. The words cut into the stone walls of the tomb, signifying real things like bread and beer, are real things themselves, more real than the bread and beer, for they remain forever and make the bread and beer endure forever too. Should the bread and beer not be offered, or should they be stolen, the words become the bread and beer and ensure they last throughout the ages.

The tomb is the first book; the house of life; the body that does not decay because it is written. Stone is cut into, cut out; this absence of stone, this concavity, this emptiness, yet means a fullness: the words appearing, their presence overcoming the absence of what they denote, filling emptiness with meaning, creating the world over and over again. Writing, I live; I enter that world beyond the false door of the tomb; my existence continues throughout eternity.

I have written my father's name, and I have written my own name underneath. I have joined them. I have enclosed them within a cartouche. My father's hand presses my shoulder. When I lift my eyes, I see him smile.

*

When I sit in the little window alcove of my attic bedroom, working out recipes at the table you have built for me from a chopped door on trestles, my eyes are level with rooftops, blue-grey slopes of slate. When it rains they shine like mussels. This morning, in the dry misty light of September, they have a dull gleam; soon the moist sun will break through. An eye of a window, curtained with thin strips of grey and yellow chintz, stares back at me. The gardens below are invisible this high up. Between me and the house opposite is a packed space of crisp air, the top of the sycamore tree. My eye darts through the narrow gap between two houses: tarmac, the heel of a yellow car, a slice of pavement. Beyond the triple rows of windows braced by black drainpipes, more grey roofs and fat red chimney pots, and behind them again a crest of green, the start of the grey sky.

Not *your* bedroom, you correct me: *ours*.

The bed is wide and low, facing the window hung with thick blue cloth. The enormous mirrors you salvaged from a fairground lean against one wall; sometimes I look up from lovemaking and watch us ride each other like merry-go-round horses on striped poles, white arses flashing up down, up down. A smallish room whose roof slopes in two directions. Behind the head of the bed, a door. I know it's a second attic, but I haven't cleaned it out yet. One day soon I'm going to drag the bed aside, open that door, explore what's within. A platform of air; a bird's nest balanced on a web of wind, containing magpie treasures. Or the tight coil of a fire escape fleeing downwards into the dark street. Or another house, a secret one twinned with this, invisible mirror-image.

I've stripped and scrubbed the walls, floor and ceiling, painted them white, but darkness still comfortably shadows the corners. I've painted the old iron bedstead bright blue, arranged a row of tin Chinese plates stencilled with fruits and vegetables on the chest of drawers, arranged my china trays of earrings and bracelets in front of them. Your cufflinks and loose change share a big yellow Pernod ashtray with my watch and brooches, just as outside, on the tiny landing, in the doorless wardrobe, my dresses and skirts interleave your trousers and jackets. On the mantelpiece my brightly painted wooden cockerel stands next to your collection of old cricket balls. On the chair, the black forest of your clean socks, my pink bathtowel, your week's worth of dirty shirts. My hairs trail from your brush and your handkerchiefs always end up under my pillow. An intimacy I haven't known before, that I sometimes fear.

This morning you woke up laughing. You strolled about shaving, hunting for a T-shirt, getting dressed, while I lay in bed drinking the tea you brought me and reading the newspaper. You ironed your shirt while I struggled with the crossword. You came back to bed, lay down next to me on the blue duvet, took me in your arms. Then you were racing downstairs with the rubbish sack and I heard the front door bang, your car start up. I put my head into the dent made by yours in the pillow, held the smell and the warmth you'd left behind. The ceiling in one corner is still shored up by two planks; I thought how daft I was to have painted the room before getting the builder in to fix the roof on that side. But the brown and yellow roses of the wallpaper in here stifled me, and the thick brown lino; I was impatient to make them disappear.

The sight of the typewriter on the table under the window tugged me up. I threw on yesterday's comfortable old clothes, sat down to get in three hours' work before going off to cook at the Dining Rooms. Yet I find myself blocked from writing recipes this morning. Two coats of white paint haven't covered over my memory of this room as it so recently was, walled in beige and pink and yellow roses. What was she like, I wonder, the old woman who owned this house before me and who died in the bed we sleep in? I met Miss Cotter only once; the house was put up for sale before she died; her plan was to move into a nursing home on the proceeds and end her days there. She was small and fierce; someone's daughter and granddaughter, I supposed; what does it mean to have relatives? I never let myself think of my aunt and uncle. The old woman had thick straight white hair, she wore sunglasses indoors, and she painted her nails orange. She hung on here to the end, avoiding the nursing home, the hospital bed that would soon have followed, the machines that would have prolonged her pain-filled frailty. She chose to slip off overnight when no one was watching, before the ambulance came.

I cried when I heard she was dead. I cried as though I'd known her properly, as though I'd had a grandmother. I toasted her memory in whisky.

I came again to see the house, which was mine now, to explore it, a cat going into a new box. The hall smelt of gravy and soap. I began in the basement, poking through old Ovaltine and Bisto tins, and ended up here in the attic bedroom after clambering up stairs littered with torn lampshades, old biros, broken picture-frames, the rubbish left by the dealers when they cleared the house. The old lady's relatives had taken the few bits and pieces they thought were valuable, and sold the rest. But the bed was still here on the bare floor, brown iron frame bracing a grey and yellow striped calico mattress. I perched on its edge, feeling cold, and looked at the wallpaper. Six months later I met you, and we decided to live together. Too quick, I worried. But you moved in. *My* house, I insist. *Ours*, you retort. You pay me rent. I haven't put your name on the mortgage. Not yet.

I think about that old woman as an emblem of family, I suppose. The nuns were kind enough, but they could not stop me from finding out that I was different from the other children attending the convent's school, the ones with parents, with real homes and families. I found ways of turning gritty pain to pearls: I composed fantastic stories about my exotic royal parentage, a crowned and jewelled father who would ride up with a train of elephants and camels to claim me, who would take me away to his shining white palace in a far-off country blazing with heat, who would give me a fleet of Arab stallions and a pet lion and a tame cobra, who would seat me at his right hand and never leave me again.

I wrote these stories down. I wrote in order to find out whether I had the right to exist, how real the world was, how much it touched me, whether it could include me. Words were alive like dogs and trees and made me real too; I wove nets of words which held me up. I know that the deep dark pit waits just in front of my feet; I have fallen into it often enough; but I have learned, too, about resting there at the bottom until it's time to clamber back up out. I have survived a difficult beginning, and I am lucky. I am safe now. And I have a home; even better, one that demands I work on it, to make it exactly what I want.

Yesterday I began on the bathroom. I soaked a sponge in soapy water, ran it over the ancient wallpaper, cursed as drips ran down my outstretched arm to roost coldly in my armpit. I pulled off the paper in long strips; I peeled and tore, enjoying the destruction. I washed the walls again, then scraped off the last remnants of lining paper and paste. I took off layers of history, a sodden shredded palimpsest curled under my feet. Tomorrow I shall fill in the holes in the plaster, the gaps and cracks, I shall sand down these walls whose gleaming patchiness smells of soap and ammonia, cold and sweet, I shall consider undercoat, emulsion, gloss. The antique Ascot no longer works. We took a bath together last night, our weekly one, cans of hot water carried down three flights. We lolled by candlelight, five white candles glimmering in the tall branched candelabra I found at the back of the cupboard under the stairs, black shadows lapping the chipped enamel edge of the bath, a peaceful gloom, the black evening pressing up to the dimpled glass of the window. I read out bits of a cookery book to you and you chose supper; I steamed out plaster dust with carnation bathsalts, you washed my back for me and I yours, we drank gin and tonics and listened to a sung Mass by Schütz on the radio.

Happiness has entered me, expanded me. Made me big. I am in control of my life. I have done with self-pity as I have done with being the homeless woman on the street at night, gazing at other people's lit golden windows. I have opened myself to the possibility of continuing happiness. I have done nothing to deserve happiness, and that doesn't matter; it's not a reward for being good. I've simply learned how to open up to it, how to let it in and accept it. Grace, the nuns called it. I have it now. It lives in me, it kicks and swims: my baby, who will be born in seven months' time.

Rosina and I roam the room, trying to contain restlessness in neat steps, imaginary silk trains slashing from side to side as our hands clench and lift our skimpy dresses, transforming them to ball-gowns with real bustles. We pretend we can hear the slither of lace, the linoleum-covered floor transformed to golden wood sprung for dancing and polished to satin. Back and forth, back and forth between the bureau and the bed.

But the game is unsatisfactory, hindered by the lack of a proper reflection. The looking glass, a plain square propped on top of the bureau, is too high up and too small. I stand on tiptoe, neck stretched, for a view of face and shoulders, hands coming up to hide mended frills of muslin. Near the hairtidy in flowered violet china that I hate, too bright, is some spilt face powder filched from Mother's room, delicate unbroken grains till you put your finger in it and you blend it, a pinkish smear on the wood's bloom, like my breath clouding the mirror. That's how the rouge should go on too, if we only had some to practise with. But Mother draws the line there. Her cheeks are red enough anyway.

I drop onto the bed, heavily, enjoying the way its sagging mattress receives me, the clothes tumbled there giving way under me and rising up around my collapsed body like waves, a foam of buttons and laces breaking over me. A cut plush sleeve tickles my cheek, like Rosina's eyelashes did when we played that guessing game with our eyes closed, stroking each other's faces with handkerchiefs and feathers.

The ceiling above me is cream yellowing to grey, criss-crossed by fine cracks. I pinch the coarse cotton coverlet between my fingers. Nothing is right here. Not since Father died.

Boredom is measured by the clock ticking outside on the landing. The hard edges of the room make me ache. Only another hour before Mother returns from the bazaar to check on the state of my sick headache. I can hear my own breathing, Rosie's too. Outside, the sounds of a man whistling in the empty afternoon, a dog barking, cut across the street clatter. I yawn, stretching on the heap of dressing-up things. Then Rosina's voice comes clear and sharp, making me start.

– It's your turn. You decide what to do next. Go on.

Rosina sits on the little wooden armchair at the side of the empty grate. Sits as she likes, no one to see her and fuss, one leg hoisted over the arm, shoe dangling from one arched foot, the other stretched out in front of her. I used to see my father sit like that of an evening, when he fetched a jug of beer home with him from the public house and a couple of friends too, and I was allowed to stay up a little longer before being shooed away up to bed by Mother, away from their smoking, their bursts of talk. When I was small enough not to be noticed.

I remember those male limbs, loose and relaxed. The pipe held between the red lips. The brown moustaches and beard, their softness known to me from cuddling on his lap and putting my hand up to stroke his face, explore the surfaces of bone under the furred and pitted skin. Sucking my thumb, I'm half asleep on his knee, his chest pushing in and out against me, my head pressed to his serge heart. The yellow light of the lamp falls on the round table crammed up against the window. Beat of a moth's wings. Hiss of the fire collapsing to one red quivering mass, Mother's knees tucked under the tablecloth, her spectacles on as she peers at her darning, the soft hill of stockings heaped in front of her. A sigh; I don't know why.

The visitors sit opposite my father, chairs drawn snugly to the heat, boots on the bright brass fender the fire flickers on. Foam, crusting their top lips, which they lick off. Warm in my woolly nightgown, I drowse in my father's arms, opening an eye to catch Mr Jackson settling back, hands spread over his red waistcoat belly, Mr Carling poking his pipe, suck and bubble, before putting another match to it. One ear cocked to their incomprehensible talk. How far away Mother is. Hunched over her work, thin shoulders tense as she steers thread towards the needle's eye, in her own little circle of light that the men don't need, enclosed by the red glow of the fire. The heavy curtains are drawn. Thick ones, down to the ground. Behind them, the swish of rain against the glass. I'm held against my father's heart. I slip my hand inside his jacket and feel his warmth, the steady pulse and drum of his blood, sniff the sweet rich smell of the macassar oil on his hair, the scent of coal burning, its whisper and tickle. I rest in the dark cave of his arms, lit by firelight. His fingers are stained with tobacco and ink. His body rises and falls under mine. Him wrapped round me. He and I are the world.

I'm too old for all that now. He's gone. And that was a little girl who doesn't exist any more. Too old for all that now.

The forgotten headache bangs my brow. I shiver. The room is cold. Too expensive to spend money on coal for a fire in the daytime in spring. Meagre, this room, and too light, the merciless sun outlining its tidy cleanliness that hurts me. The pink and brown roses on the wallpaper stare back, mouths that mock. I hate this house now that Father isn't in it.

Rosina strikes her hands on the arms of her chair.

– You're wasting time!

I hoist myself up onto one elbow. Consider.

– All right. First of all we've got to make it dark. Then you'll see.

We make night-time in the middle of the day. Like in winter, in late December, when night reaches far back into the day, when we have to light the gas at three o'clock to chase away the shadows. Like at Christmas, when all the relatives pile in and the little parlour crackles with gaiety. I remember the smell of hot wet cloth, the pudding boiling in the kitchen next door, the smell of punch dark and spicy with rum, choking me with its hot sweetness at the back of my throat when I'm allowed a sip from Father's glass. Holly and ivy loop along the walls, around the mirror, turning the cramped parlour into a green forest twinkling with candles and red berries. The smell of pine gusts from the tree in the corner, bendy green fronds brushing the ceiling, candles burning in its green depths.

Roast dinner and pudding at two o'clock. Afterwards, the grown ups chat and doze in the half-dark amidst a litter of walnut shells and raisin stems on the white cloth, dessert bowl of green china piled high with red apples arranged on leaves. Under the table, we children explore a dark nest woven of trouser-legs and skirts. Tired of our games here, stealing shoes and tickling stockinged feet damp with sweat, we sidle out, escape upstairs. Here, there is no light. As though we're out of the house altogether, a part of the endless night. Yet the house holds us gently in its dark arms, and it chuckles, transforming itself.

We inch our way up the steep stairs, on all fours, feeling for each cold stair-rod with fingers and toes. We crawl along the scratchy drugget on the landing, pretending to be dogs. I rub my face against my cousin's ankles then grab them and bring him down on top of me. But we mustn't make too much noise as we wrestle. We don't want to summon voices and lights from downstairs.

We huddle in my bedroom, deciding what to play. Hide and seek. No need to put our hands over our eyes; we can't see anything. Rosina melts away as we count to twenty. A hush. Then the creak of the door as my cousins leave the room one by one. I hear the rasp of their fingers along the wall, guided by it.

Alone. In the pitch darkness. Which is my home. Which I know. Which lets me expand into something, someone, larger than a child or my ordinary daily self. Full of strength, ideas, experience. My parents pretend that children of seven are just little animals to be kept clean and fed, but in the darkness I outwit them, grow up, very tall, full of secret knowledge. In the cocoon of darkness. Breathing slowly and deeply in and out. I've given up my eyes; I don't need them. The darkness touches me, velvet on my face and wrists, and I dissolve into it. So that I can flow about the room, a dark cloud skimming a dark sky, a dark fish swimming in dark water, released from my skin, free to be part of what was formerly outside me but which now enters and melts me like chocolate, or mud. I'm a dark ooze swirling and spreading, no boundaries, no tight clothes to hold me in, to hold me back. I'm liquid darkness rolling over the rug, under the bed.

Dust scratches my nostrils. The bedsprings coil near my face, the coverlet falls like a curtain. A knowledge of objects I notice with regret, it means I'm coming back in to myself, darkness reforming and compressing me to make me a person again, a body with eyes all over, a body that can somehow see, in the stuffy blackness, Rosina curled up, as far away as she can get, in the angle of the wall. Perhaps I see in the dark by smelling? Rosie must have heard me tumble in, but the game is to give no sign. I hear her trying not to breathe.

Thick air between us, of no words, tingling, a sort of wall, or blanket. Delicately, finger by finger, toe by toe, I crawl further in, close to Rosina, touch her hand. Our special sign: my thumb circling her palm. Then I fit myself close to my sister, taking up the space of air next to her, empty till I arrive to fill it. I wait, absorbing Rosie's silence, my mouth on her hair, my arm round her. In the daytime you can't get this close. So you can't lose yourself either. Only in the dark. We settle into each other, a comfortable mix of arms and knees, and listen for footsteps returning from other rooms.

That little girl has gone too. Lost forever. Daylight replaces her, is the serious time. Work. Night is only for sleeping, sometimes for highly-coloured dreams. I'm sixteen now, almost grown-up. Tomorrow I'll put up my thick yellow hair and become an infant school teacher. Dogsbody and drudge more like, wiping runny noses, messes on the floor. Better than going into service like Mother did, as she keeps reminding me.

Rosina draws the bedroom curtains. A rattle and a click, a thin swish. She makes night happen. In the nearly dark, her figure hovers by the bed. My sister's been apprenticed to a dressmaker. She's lucky too.

– So get up, Flora. And tell me the game we're going to play.

When the grown ups wake from their naps, we have tea: pink slices of boiled ham, bread and butter and watercress, custard tarts sprinkled with nutmeg, fruit cake covered with marzipan stuck with sugar roses, mince pies. Then the candles are lit on the little piano, the sheet music fetched and propped on the stand that folds out like a gate, my father settles himself on the plush-covered stool, spreading his hands over the yellowing keys. He's got a real gift, Mother says, but there's never time except at Christmas.

Now Aunt Dolly steps forward, centre stage, her hands clasped over her lace jabot that heaves up and down with the effort of getting her voice out high and pure. Her two chins wobble. Rude music hall ditties she sings, that have all the adults in red-faced laughter, tender love songs that have them looking comically, tenderly, at each other. I'm embarrassed by my parents spooning in public, her arm going around his shoulders as he plays for her, grins at her. I look away. Aunt Dolly towers on the hearthrug, the light on her hair, her eyes closed, and she's no longer Aunt Dolly, fat feet jammed into tight boots, blouse straining, but a river of gold, a prima donna singing out power.

Just sitting together in the dark, Rosie-Posy, holding hands and wishing. In the lovely warm blessed dark, waiting to see what will happen. Whether I can get lost, and then what I'll find.

Your latest letter, my darling Mamma, has not a little disturbed me, I must confess. Indeed I wept upon reading it. Most humbly I submit myself, of course, to your superior judgment and experience, and for your advice I am, as you know, always grateful. Yet I fear that you have misunderstood the situation and that your anxiously affectionate heart, so keen to promote your children's wellbeing and protect their interests, may have leapt ahead of your reason in this instance, thereby forming too hastily, and may I say, unadvisedly, a painful conclusion.

Allow me to remind you, dearest Mamma, that my husband must be the judge of my actions. He stands between me and the world; he is my counsellor and my guide. Where William can see no harm, I walk freely and unafraid, extending the hand of friendship where and as I choose. My husband approves my friendship with Miss and Mr Andrews, so why should not you? How like my dear worrying old Mamma to get herself into a fret!

She must be guided sometimes by her little Minny's knowledge of the ways of the great world. In Surrey, no doubt, different rules may apply. But here in London we may dare to be cosmopolitan and bold, and to make new acquaintances as the impulses of the heart, and not merely the dictates of convention, suggest.

As for Miss Milk, it was William's express wish that I should extend her my patronage. I of course immediately complied. It is impossible to suspect one so young, innocent and beautiful of deceitful intent, and I am, I must say, shocked that you have allowed your mind to entertain such dark thoughts of one who is not only pure as an angel and incapable of falsehood, but whose conduct has been readily submitted to the calm and objective scrutiny of William himself. As a scientist he is not easily misled. Money, my dear Mamma, is not Flora's object. Hers, she has stressed to me, is comparable to a religious vocation. Her gift is enacted, and bears its fruit, high above the level of miserable pecuniary gain, even though it has, unfortunately, become linked to the necessity, for Flora, of having to earn her living outside the bosom of her family. Her father having died a year ago, the family is in difficult straits. Mr Milk seems to have been sadly improvident in not laying by a goodly proportion of his earnings against the possibility of his early demise. This having been the case, Flora must augment the meagre pension her mother receives.

It is, I must say, deeply troubling to me that young mediums should have to expose themselves in public, on platforms, at meetings open to all sorts of riff-raff choosing to avail themselves of the spectacle of a lovely young girl speaking in tongues. All earnest seekers after the truth must feel, as William does, that a medium secures most respect, and is most protected from any threat of exploitation, by practising her calling solely in private, amongst a company of affectionate and supportive friends. I take an interest in little Flora, and I scruple not to add that my interest is deepened by my knowledge of William's growing conviction that she is enabled by some mysterious power to bring us messages from our loved ones who have passed on. Under these circumstances it is understandable that I should wish to help her, not least by encouraging her to shun the evil of appearing in public in order to secure the patronage of dubious wellwishers. I *intend* to go to one of her seances! You cannot, my dearest

Mamma, wish me to refuse the blessing of receiving some consolation for the death of little Rosalie!

Forgive me, Mamma! I have been so unwell since receiving your last letter that it is easy for me to react over-emotionally to subjects such as this one that affects me so deeply. You know how sadly passionate is my nature. Believe me, I will endeavour to check it, for in my present state of health I must endeavour to remain calm and sedate. Simply, I beg you to trust me when I tell you that little Flora's gifts are in no sense un-Christian and in no way depart from the eternal truths taught by the Church. Indeed, they *add* to our knowledge of that Mystery of Resurrection contained in the New Testament; they confirm it. And God-fearing scientists such as William deem it part of their noble undertaking to ascertain whether the practices of mediums such as little Flora, carefully tested under the most stringent conditions, may not aid us more fully to penetrate the great secrets of life and death. But this is William's terrain; in this field I do not pretend to be competent. For my own part, I am satisfied as a grieving and suffering mother if I may be enabled to receive the inexpressible comfort of learning that my lost loved little one is alive and happy beyond the grave. May no one wrest that from me! William and the children send you, of course, all their love.

Ever your affectionate daughter,
Minny.

Our life is one long preparation for our death, to ensure that our life after death is as joyous as the one we know before it. The ceremonies attending the death of a King are wrapped in mystery; the ancient rituals that prepare him for eternal life are performed and witnessed only by the priests, deep in the recesses of the mortuary temples. Yet my father, who on his death will join the gods and become one of them, considers it part of my education that I should understand a little of what will happen when he dies, in order better to prepare myself for my great future. He forces me to contemplate his death, which will be a new beginning for both of us.

The servants have carried our chairs outside and set them in my garden in the shade of the fig tree. My hair is still wet after my bathe; my body aches pleasurably in the warm air. My hunger can be satisfied by the fruit hidden in the dark green depths of the tree, my thirst by the cup of wine I hold between my hands. Nothing of this will be altered by death. I shall be closer to my father than before.

The process of preparing his body for burial, my father tells me, will take seventy days.

First, his body will be laid on a reed mat, outside in the sun, and heaped with powdered natron, to dry it out.

It will be washed free of excess salt with Nile water, a ritual lustration which symbolizes the rising of the sun from the Nile and the subsidence of the flood waters. Now it will be brought back inside.

The embalmers will don their masks of the gods. The chief embalmer will wear the jackal mask of Anubis.

The head will be anointed, and then the rest of the body.

To remove the brain from the skull, a chisel will be inserted into one nostril in order to break through the bone there into the cavity surrounding the brain and to enable the tissue to be extracted with an iron probe. The empty skull will then be refilled with linen steeped in resin.

The nostrils will be sealed with linen soaked in resin, and the ears will be closed in the same way.

If the eyes have fallen out, new ones will be made and inserted into the eye sockets.

A vertical incision will be made in the left side of the abdomen, and the viscera pulled out. The interior of the abdomen will be washed and anointed, then re-packed with resinous linen. To do this properly, the skin of the trunk must be separated from the muscular tissue underneath to allow the introduction of the linen pads beneath the skin of the chest and back. Cuts made at the shoulders allow the arms to be packed, and cuts across the heels allow this for the feet.

Sawdust and mud will fill the body. The wounds made by the embalmers will be stitched up.

The viscera will be placed in four Canopic jars inside a coffer fitting tightly round them. At its corners will stand the guardian goddesses Isis, Nepthys, Neith and Selkis, their wings extended, their fingertips touching each other's.

The skin around the fingernails will be cut, to protect the skin loosened during the embalming, and the fingers will be wrapped while spells are recited to restore to my father the use of his hands and feet.

The head will receive its final anointing, before being wrapped in bandages impregnated in oils and resin, with amulets inserted between the layers. Now my father will never be deprived of his head in the next world.

The hands and arms will be treated with oils and resin, then wrapped. Protective amulets will be placed between the linen bandages.

Finally, the legs will be treated and wrapped in the same way, and the recitation by the priest will confirm that my father has regained the use of his legs.

My father's body will have been made whole again, just as the dismembered and scattered body of Osiris was searched for and collected up by Isis in order to be given burial.

All the parts of my father will be held together inside his linen bandages. His body will be made new.

My father will rise, to join the gods. I shall rise too, and search for him, in the heavens, and find him there. I shall climb up the rays of the sun. I shall sit next to him, for ever. He will never leave me again.

This morning, when I dashed out to buy more polyfilla, the rain had just stopped and the air was still full of moisture, like steam. The leaves on the plane trees were a bright grey-green, while the leaves fallen onto the ground were scorched brown, scarlet, lime-green, a thick dark yellow. The washed stone slabs of the pavement leapt up at me: olive, turquoise, lavender, pink. One parked car was a shout of crimson, another of electric blue. A scrap of purple tinfoil gleamed on a flight of steps leading to a rust front door. A brick wall was ochre and coffee and black, streaked with scarlet and bright yellow. I could taste every colour in my mouth, as I could taste the bitter rotting leaves and the bonfire smoke from back gardens and the blue plastic sacks of refuse leaning against a warehouse door. I brought some of the colours home with me: a ragged bunch of dahlias and chrysanthe-mums, dark red, pink, russet, salmon. The tawny colours of peaches and nectarines, the colours of earth on a hillside, the baked clay, the pots and dishes made from it to hold vegetables and fruit. Italian colours: sombre rose, grey, terracotta.

The bathroom wall was a dingy pink. The plaster was pitted, porous, in some places cracked, in others loose. Sometimes when I tapped it, it fell away in dry powdery lumps and flakes. I knocked on the walls as though someone slept behind them and needed waking, as though the wall were a door that would swing open on its hinges and let me through. I discovered that instead the wall was fragile, a weave merely of lath and plaster, and hastily stopped encouraging it to fall down. I dipped my palette knife into the pot in my hand, swept it over the cracks, the gaps. This superfine polyfilla was new to me, a joy to work with, smooth and elastic, going on easily, a plastic cream that magically made all blemishes in the surface vanish. Such pleasure to pass my knife over the gaping holes, fill them exactly and quickly one by one, silkily fitting softness into the gaps in solidity, from edge to edge, until all was solid, the walls perfectly smooth, and white lines and circles were memories of the cracks, mapping them. An erotic pleasure: to press into the containing crevices of the walls and fill their emptiness, over and over again, to make up what was lacking, to join *something* with *nothing*.

Last night I dreamed of my baby. She lay in the bath, completely immersed in the water which enclosed her like a transparent coffin. She was like the paperweight on my desk, a round dry head of thistledown, gold-white, enclosed in a clear globe of solid perspex. Her eyes were open and alert, and she watched me climb the ladder to test the soundness of the ceiling stained with rings of damp. She did not move; the water in the bath was still and undisturbed; the water lay on her eyes which looked at me. I backed down the ladder and leaned over the bath to lift her out. She was tiny and light; newborn; her skin was red and creased. I folded a thick towel around her as she lay across my lap, and patted her dry. Then I leaned over the side of the bath and pulled the plug to let the water out.

The nuns believed in the healing and cleansing efficacies of holy water. Just inside the convent chapel porch, let into the stone wall, was a great fluted half-shell, crusted, ancient. We dipped our fingers into the clear puddle in its brown depths, crossed ourselves, went to our places to pray. It was unimaginable to enter the chapel without performing this rite; like not wearing a black veil, not genuflecting. There was another stoup of holy water in the dormitory; the fervent sprinkled their beds against the assaults of the Devil in lascivious dreams. The water could be ordinary tap water, blessed by the chaplain, but the holiest sort was brought back from remote mountainous sites graced by the Virgin with miraculous springs, like Lourdes. There was yet another holy water stoup in the kitchen; Sister Bridget cooled her fingertips in it before concentrating on her shortcrust pastry.

For the nuns, an unbaptized baby was in a condition of spiritual nakedness, illness and danger; we were instructed that if ever we happened to be around a newborn, unbaptized baby, we should rectify matters with whatever water was to hand, lemonade if necessary, even spittle at a pinch. The one dream of heroism my childhood offered me: to snatch a baby from the jaws of Hell.

Older babies were paid for, a penny at a time, as our contributions to the Missions. The paper dolls representing them were moved gradually up a grand staircase, a penny per stair; at the top, in Heaven, the grand total of two and sixpence, stood Jesus, his arms outstretched to receive and bless his new child. I saw the invisible Devil chasing the children up the stairs; his slippers slid on the lino and he breathed heavily, his breath smelled of beer. Having saved my babies from the Devil, I chose their baptismal names: Sebastian, Oliver, Nicholas, Gabrielle, Frederica, Marie-Louise. The paper child was cut out of Africa and stuck onto a new white page. The nuns exhorted us to have as many babies as possible, to whiten Africa as much as possible. I wanted to be a paper baby with a new name, safe in a paper Heaven.

I shan't have my baby baptized since I don't believe in original sin any longer. But we'll hold a naming party here, to welcome the baby amongst our friends. What needs exorcizing is not the Devil out of my child but the noises out of this house.

As soon as I began to admit that I desired you, I discovered, unwillingly, my capacity for telepathy. Our closeness is a string joining us, that we tug on when we're apart. Also it's an openness, defences down, all our doors and windows standing wide to welcome each other's thoughts. I always know when you're about to return home after you've been away on a driving job; I catch myself jumping up and going over to the window to be delighted by your advance up the path. I know when you're in trouble; as though you call out. Often I know what you're about to say before you say it, or we catch ourselves both beginning to say the same thing. An invasion of my privacy, I sometimes think. I don't always want you that close. It frightens me.

Now, at night, I sometimes wake up to the sound of weeping, faint and desolate, and, if you're home, have to burrow against your warm back for comfort, turn you around so that I can wriggle into your arms and put my face against yours as you sleep. If I'm alone I put my fingers in my ears. I could be dreaming it, I suppose; certainly, you haven't heard it on the two occasions when I've woken you, insisting you listen.

Sometimes when I'm alone here of an evening, sitting reading by the fire in the sitting room, I hear footsteps walking up and down in the bedroom overhead; when I run to check, I find no one there. Sometimes, at twilight, I'll be coming downstairs and I'll catch a flicker of something, or someone, in step just behind me in the blue shadows. Once there was suddenly a strong scent of violets on the little top landing outside our room; it lingered for a few moments, then vanished, and I immediately felt very cold. It didn't alarm me. And it felt far less intrusive than the number of phone calls I get each week which turn out to be wrong numbers.

I don't believe in ghosts. There was supposed to be one at the convent, but I never caught a glimpse of her. The building in which we were housed was part of an ornate mid-Victorian terrace in Bayswater, looking over a square. Though there was therefore no scope for walled-up mediaeval nuns, the older girls would tell incoming first years about the mad lady in blue who haunted the first floor at dusk, walking up and down the corridor rocking an invisible baby. I didn't believe them. Their tale was too clearly part of an initiation rite designed to bully the little girls into submission: you ran errands for the prefects and they protected you.

I refuse to believe there is a ghost in this house, but I am curious. You don't believe in ghosts either. You're tolerant of my accounts of feeling haunted, just as you're tolerant of my dislike of answering the telephone, my need always to be able to see the door in whichever room I'm in, my recurrent nightmare of the burglar who tiptoes upstairs in slippered feet and whispers to me to hush. It's no more odd to you that I should sleep with a kitchen knife under my pillow than that you should drive a lorry part-time to earn the money to buy canvases, than that you should enjoy wearing filthy ripped trousers and digging your fingers into paint and watching boxing on television and dancing to rock n' roll. You reach for me, wrap your arms around me, kiss me. You think I'm normal. You don't think I'm mad. If there *are* ghosts here, you'll be interested.

September is my favourite month. As the year gathers itself up to start dying it crackles with energy. The early morning sky is cool grey mist, all colour bleached out, then by nine o'clock a dry sparkle breaks through, the frostiness promises heat to come, the white cloud melts to gold. Rosina and I on top of the omnibus huddle inside our thick wraps, our faces stung by wind, struck by sun. The air is crisp and sweet as toffee, the chestnut trees on Newington Green yellowing at their edges like the pages of old books. Bright asters and dahlias bristle on the flower-stall. When we get off the windy bus and stand still on the pavement for a minute we feel the season's warmth on us like a strong hand, and lift our faces to it. Then we're off arm in arm towards the market.

We've discussed the dress many times. Stylish as well as respectable, easy to move in though well-fitted, warm enough to withstand the chill of draughty meeting rooms. Rosina insists it must be black. The soft darkness of childhood solid about me. We dodge along the drapers' stalls, pinching the rolls of silk, crêpe, wool, between our fingers, holding up breadths against each other to try the effect. Finally we choose a good cotton velvet in rich black with a close deep pile, some black fake jet buttons, some black braid for trimmings. This is my first real new dress, chosen and paid for by myself. No more of Mother's and Aunt Dolly's hand-me-downs badly altered and taken in, fooling no one. Pleasure puffs me up like a pigeon. Waiting for the stall-holder to tie my parcel, I lean on a bale of printed cotton, wishing I could afford to go to a good dressmaker, have my velvet made up properly. Rosina will sew it for me; I've promised to pay her out of my next earnings.

The smell of ham frying drifts past, tickles our nostrils and our appetites, makes us turn our heads towards each other and grin. There's plenty of money left from what Rosina has lent me for the treat we've planned: a slap-up dinner. Father's watch that he left to Rosie fetched a good price at the pawnbroker's. Of course we haven't told Mother that. I forced Rosie to sell it. So sweet, my little sister. She does what I want.

Parcel under my arm, I stroll after Rosina. The dirtyish bit of white rabbit fur around her neck fills me with sudden anger. One day I'll buy her a proper mantle with a fur collar, and a hat to match. Today I've bought her a tin brooch and a little picture of a bird in a plush frame. Today we haven't quarrelled once about her wanting to be a medium too. Knowing that she hasn't got it in her makes her furious. Her future is hitched to mine now in another way, and she knows it, so she's treating me with care.

In the Hannibal Dining Rooms in Hannibal Street we find Mr Potson already there waiting for us. He twitches with relief when he sees us, darts forward to shake hands. We sit opposite him on the worn bench fastened against the wall, and settle to ordering food. Stewed beef for him, tripe and onions for me, kidneys and peas for Rosina. Looking at the buttery black squash of mushrooms he pushes uninterestedly around his plate I wish I dared offer to help him finish them. These days I'm always hungry. But I'm on my best behaviour today, speaking only when spoken to, wiping my mouth after every mouthful for fear of grease on my chin, keeping my hands on my lap once I've finished. He's bought us beer; I drink mine too fast and have to suppress burps, then giggles as I catch Rosina's eye.

– You're very young, Miss Milk, Mr Potson addresses me: for this great work. Are you sure your mother does not object? She would not prefer to see you settled at some more obviously respectable trade?

– I'm older than I look, sir, I venture: and Mother doesn't mind. She's glad I've found the work I've been born to do. She says I've improved ever so much, since finding I could do it. I'm far less trouble, she says.

He nods, grinding on a bit of gristle. He eats with his mouth open. There's a soft lake of grease, like a cold sore, on his lower lip. I look away, around me. The Dining Rooms are painted a glistening brown. The front wall, opening directly onto the street, is all plain glass panels divided by frames of sticky brown wood, that make me think of chestnuts, and the frosted glass door is propped open, exchanging the steam and smell of cooking for the cheerful hubbub of the street, streams of light and air. Men saunter in, caps over one eye, hands in pockets, lean on the counter to give their orders, seat themselves at the long benches.

One winks at me; I pretend not to see. I like this place: I'm half out on the street, it feels like, what with the sun warm through the glass and the scent of hot straw and horses drifting in from the brewery stables on the corner, and I'm half in a dark cave rattling with pots and kettles, a canary chirruping in one corner in a blue wooden cage.

Mr Potson mops up his plate at last. Bread in his hand soaked and blackened with meat juice.

– So, Miss Milk, let's get down to business, shall we?

– After my pudding, sir, if I may.

I order suet roll with butter and sugar. Rosina tucks in to an apple dumpling with custard sauce. I didn't use to fancy my meals, not for years. I was Mother's despair. Now I'm making up for it.

– Rarely, Mr Potson informs me: have I seen a young lady medium eat with such healthy enjoyment as you, Miss Milk. Rarely.

He wags his head sorrowfully to and fro. He himself is pale and thin, his skin greeny-white. He's as delicate-looking as an artistic sort of hero in a novel. He has lank curling chestnut hair and moustaches and he's constantly fingering his chin, where a wisp of beard is beginning. His fingernails are certainly not as clean as mine.

– I've got to keep my strength up, sir, I protest, just to tease him: it's hard and tiring work getting those chairs and tables to fly up and down!

– Hush, he cautions me: quietly, if you please. Anyone overhearing you, my dear Miss Milk, could easily misunderstand your words. Suspicion, on the part of the public, as you already know, is something we must always be on our guard against.

I put down my spoon.

– Well, sir. I've thought over your offer very carefully and I should like to accept it. That is, for a trial period of three months. After that, I think we should review the situation.

– Three months is a very short time, my dear, he hazards: to study in depth all that there is to know about our great calling. For a comparatively new science it has already gathered to itself an enormous amount of written material. This will take you some time to absorb.

– Oh, I'm a very fast reader, I tell him, starting to gather up my things preparatory to going: and in any case I don't have to be a scholar to be a good medium, do I? It's the practical side that counts. The breathing and relaxation. And all the other things.

– Quite so.

He's watching me and Rosina pull on our gloves. He twiddles his necktie and shoots his cuffs.

– And the fee? he blurts: do you agree to my terms?

– Ten per cent, I announce: of all my earnings over three months, and not a penny more. My mother's not able to work these days. We'll need all the money I make. And I'm sure I'll make plenty if I learn from you, sir!

He eyes me uneasily. I beam at him, and wait.

– Very well, then, he mutters: ten per cent it is.

We pay for our dinners and depart. Jubilation held inside plops out as laughter only when we're round the corner and out of sight. I hurry Rosina past stalls heaped with second-hand hats. No dawdling: I need all my spare time now for practising.

Our house snuffs out the sunlight, brings us back under control. Its narrow hallway sorts and organizes our unruly legs and arms, just like the pews in chapel comb the congregation into respectable order. The air in the hall is thick and brown, a soup of gloom. It's composed of my mother's tears, her suppressed shouts, my father's defeat by illness and death, my mother's worry about making do. We unpin our hats, take them off, lay them on the tiny half-moon table behind the front door, sidle through the hall holding our breath in case Mother hears us from upstairs and shouts for us, then clatter down the steep wooden stairs to the kitchen.

The kitchen is everyone's room. Perhaps because of the range there that helps heat the whole house. The kitchen keeps us alive, warm, fed. It's the place where we get to know one another. It's the place where Mother sets Rosie and me to work, washing and scrubbing. I am intimate with the cracks between the floorboards, with the underneath of chair seats, with the tops of cupboards; I have scraped dirt and dust from all of them. I know exactly how the wood on the windowsill is rotting year by year, aided by my bored fingernails which pick at it, prise off thick soft splinters.

Mother must be asleep. The little ones are still at school. Rosina and I sit down on opposite sides of the kitchen table. For the moment the flags on the floor are unmuddied by dirty boots, the shelves of the dresser do not need wiping, the kettle does not demand polishing, the blue and white cups and plates are clean and dry, no drops of grease soil the stove, the tap above the sink glitters and is still, the dust halts in its advance. Half an hour to ourselves, before Mother wakes up, the children run in, the messiness of family life begins again. A clean kitchen in the middle of the afternoon; sanded and quiet; empty except for us two who don't disturb anything.

I can't afford a ouija board. Instead, I use a glass, and pieces of cardboard on which I've written the letters of the alphabet in the elegant capitals my father taught me so long ago to form. His hand guiding mine to add a flourish of serifs, his hand closing round mine, holding it within his, his index finger pushing mine. His spirit hovering behind me now perhaps, as the familiar chill settles on my shoulders like a wide collar even before I've finished laying out the bits of card in as exact a circle around the upended glass as I can make.

The glass jerks.

Under my fingertips, which barely touch it, there's a skipping, a dance. A ballet in cheap glass, a dancer in a transparent dress.

I try to remember Mr Potson's instructions, the question to ask first. But I'm frightened that my voice will disturb whatever's happening, break the glass or the contact, and so my words come out in a squeak. I cough, to clear my throat, and start again.

– Which spirit is this? Will you tell us your name?

The glass knocks back and forth between the shiny cards, the big black letters.

HA. HA. HA. HA! HA HA!

Opposite me, my sister frowns and shrugs. I shrug back at her, and my answering frown, the mirror image of hers, means: let's have another go.

HAT. HAT.

– Don't tease me, please, I beg: I'm serious. I want to know who you are.

The glass slows its crazy progress back and forth, darts to the same letters as before, hesitates, then completes a new word.

HATTIE.

Our silence is taut, two indrawn breaths in the same second. I bow my head, to hide from Rosina the triumph that must show in my face and which I should not feel. I've waited weeks for this. The first time I've made contact with a spirit who has a name and is willing to give it. Not because you're ready for it, Mr Potson cautioned me: not because you've proved yourself or prepared yourself, no, you're not worthy and you never will be, none of us is, you must be humble at each tiny step you take along the great road. By the grace of God.

But simple joy is allowed, surely.

– Hallo Hattie, I say: Welcome.

HALLO FLORA.

I look at Rosina. She's nodding at me: go on.

– Who are you, Hattie? Who were you, when you were alive down here?

FARE. O! FARE.

– Fair? You were beautiful?

Rosie waggles her fingers. The glass tries again.

FARE. O! FARE.

– Yes, beautiful, I repeat: beautiful.

The glass is irritated at my stupidity. It starts again, darting back and forth across the circle of cards.

HATTIE. KING. HATTIE KING.

I lift my fingertips off the glass, cheerful and aching.

– Hattie King! You're called Hattie King!

I massage my wrists, then flex them. Mother calls from upstairs. The glass jumps up from the centre of the table, flies to the edge, teeters there, then topples off and shatters on the floor.

Well, dearest Mamma, I have at long last attended my first seance, and very moving, perplexing and consoling it was. How much I should like to tell you all about it, in order to share with you my joy at discovering that death is *not* the end, that the grave does *not* triumph, that there are secrets of life beyond this vale of tears that a poor little girl from Hackney (of all places!) is equipped by God's merciful power to disclose! And indeed I *shall* set it all down here, for the tenor of your most recent letter is such as to suggest that you are ready, nay eager, to follow your griefstricken daughter along the new pathway of hope that has opened up in front of her. Believe me, Mamma, your change of heart has done *me* so much good, in enabling me to admire and revere afresh that tolerance and open-mindedness in you which has let you admit that your troubled and difficult daughter, so long the object of your unfailing concern, may yet have something to teach her wise old mother. You have made me feel newly gathered to your heart, and that I am forgiven all the rashness and impetuosity with which I dared to speak to you of my new discoveries.

But I digress. Let me straightaway recount to you, without any more loss of time, the strange and thrilling events of last Tuesday evening, in the belief that you trust your little Minny to be making her account as sober and factual as she can, her memory unclouded by vain wishes and her judgment unimpaired by hasty emotion. My pulse is calm (I have just got Nurse to take it) and my heartbeat likewise; yet what I have to impart would make the steadiest nerves shriek aloud! Most surprising, is it not, that someone of my extreme sensibility, so long prostrate with shattering sorrow, should prove herself rock steady and cold as ice when confronted with the awful mysteries of Death? Yet so it transpired.

You must know then that William accompanied me to the little house in Clarence Road which I formerly described, where the Milk family resides, for, as he observed, it was not right that I should visit such an insalubrious neighbourhood (inhabited, he tells me, mainly by respectable clerks and their families and other people of that class, but *so close* to those eastern districts where vice and squalor abound) unaccompanied, nor did he wish to be absent on my first occasion of discovering for myself little Flora's powers of mediumship after contenting myself for so long, as I had done hitherto, with the calm sagacity of his own account. No: William had decided that it was high time I made my own experiment, divined for myself the full wonder of the little medium's potential. Also, of course, he wished to attend on his own account, for his researches into Miss Milk's capabilities are only just begun.

With my dear husband at my side, therefore, I had nothing to fear. We were a small company, fortunately I daresay, for any large number of observers would have been seriously incommoded in that pokey little kitchen where, so surprisingly, the spirits insist on being received. Mrs Milk I knew from my previous visit; there were no others present of my acquaintance. I was introduced to Mr James Hadbury, the President of the Hackney Psychical Association, who had the happy fortune to draw little Flora's powers to the notice of the scientific world, to a student, Mr Charles Young, whom I understand to be writing a doctoral thesis on the psychology of the phenomena we were about to witness, and to two very respectable-looking women, whose names I have forgot, who are neighbours of the Milk family. A young person whom I had hoped to meet but who was sadly absent, being indisposed with a bad cold, was Miss Rosina Milk, Flora's younger sister.

Little Flora (such I *must* style her, *Miss Milk* seeming too formal an address for one of her youth and charm) bowed and shook hands with all of us before her mother conducted us to our seats – the hardest of wooden chairs – at one end of the kitchen. It is her custom not to speak immediately before a seance, so that she may save her voice for the spirits' sole use. For similar reasons, I daresay, we were not offered any refreshment, this being, after all, more of a religious occasion than a social call. Mrs Milk, once we were all settled, disclosed to our notice what I had not remarked before: a large cabinet built into the far corner of the kitchen, made of solid oak, of the sort normally used, I would imagine, for the storage of kitchen brooms and mops and the like. Its interior made vacant, it now served as a cabinet for the medium; for although Flora began her career by becoming involved with receiving spirit messages through the medium of their rapping and rocking the kitchen table at which she sat, she has now progressed so far as to be able to dispense with such gross channels of communication, having discovered that she has been endowed with the capacity to undergo full spirit possession.

Into this cabinet's interior, as I say, Mrs Milk now proposed to introduce her daughter. First of all though, in the rigorous interests of scientific enquiry, she wished us to ascertain that she concealed nothing about her on her person or in her clothing that might give rise to the suspicion of trickery. To this end therefore she requested that her daughter be closely searched by one of the ladies of the party. As the most senior lady in the room, and as one with, I must confess, my curiosity already keenly whetted, I immediately advanced and offered my services. Conveying little Flora into the adjoining room – the aforementioned 'parlour' – I caused her to allow me to examine her as minutely as her modesty made possible. This examination she bore with the stoical indifference so typical of the females of her class, *their* notions of modesty being so different to *ours*. Under her black velvet dress, made, I was glad to see, in the simplest of fashions as befits her youth and her situation, my eye could discern no places of concealment: no pockets in her chemise, no false hems in her petticoat. She wore no stays, which not a little surprised me, until her mother, who stood by to witness the operation, explained to me that whalebone and tight lacing severely impeded the deep breathing necessary to her daughter's entering the trance state, whereupon I was forced to conclude the good sense of this otherwise unconventional mode of dress. Flora's form, I must say, is most charming; it is that of a nymph in a painting. Her skin is white and unblemished by scars of any sort, her waist is small, her limbs in perfect proportion. Her hair and teeth are likewise good: long, fair and abundant in the former case, small, white and even in the latter. Shall I confess to you that the sight of her maidenly charms gave me no small pleasure, confirming as they did her indisputable beauty of soul? Inconceivable that evil should dwell behind that fair countenance, that soft breast! And her underclothes, I must confess it surprised me to discover, similarly testified to her unimpeachable moral status, being as clean and exquisite as my own.

We now returned to the kitchen, where I was able to satisfy the company of Flora's innocence of any artificial aids. All about her is indeed so *real*, but then, dearest Mamma, I hope that you may yet discover that for yourself on your next visit to us. We took our places as before, while Mr Hadbury placed Flora inside the cabinet, tied her securely with ropes to her chair, and invited William to inspect the resultant knots. This he duly did, pronouncing them so firm as to be unloosable by any human agency he knew of. Mr Hadbury then sealed them. The door was then closed and locked, the key being ceremonially handed to William for custody. Now the gas was extinguished so that, as we sat behind drawn curtains, the room was almost totally in darkness. I forgot to say that before the gas was lowered the floor in front of the cabinet was liberally sprinkled with flour.

Now the seance began, with a hymn in which we all joined, and a heartfelt prayer, uttered by Mr Hadbury, for divine guidance and protection, after which we sat, meditating, in silence, each person clasping the hands of his neighbours on either side of him. William sat on my left (his fingers so cool and steady over my little fluttering hand!) and Mrs Milk on my right, *her* grip being characterized by a certain roughness and leatheriness, to say nothing of excessive warmth. I believe she was a washer-woman, or something of that sort, at one time. Only imagine, dearest Mamma, your little Minny in such company! They are a very good sort of people, I daresay; certainly her mother has Flora's interests much at heart. You will fancy me grown quite radical, I fear, to be sitting down with persons of the servant class. Only it is indisputable that the spirits are great levellers, in a way that normally one would not quite wish. Still, the solemnity of the occasion enabled me to bear the close proximity of *serge* and *carbolic* with reasonable equanimity. I will confess, too, that the tearful longings threatening to gush forth from my breast in a hearty outburst of tears were not unmixed with sentiments of deep awe and frightful apprehension; under these circumstances it was not unpleasant to be placed near the solid form of Mrs Milk and to have my hand so firmly clasped by hers; she is a motherly sort of woman after all, and not incapable, I afterwards perceived, of feeling just as she ought about sacred subjects.

We sat thus for perhaps thirty minutes. It was of course impossible for me to consult my watch. Next to me William breathed steadily, Mrs Milk more stertorously. Someone, Mr Young I think, was seized by a fit of coughing (you see how exact I am trying to make my account!). I began to grow sleepy, and my arms and wrists to ache. Abandoning all pretensions to being granted the comfort I had come to seek, I began to pray to the Almighty, in the simplest and most childlike words I could summon up within my heart, to grant me the spirit of resignation with regard to the loss of my child. At that very moment we all started, our eager attention inescapably caught by the sound of a thump in the region of the cabinet. I was not frightened, for William had warned me previously that the spirits invariably made their presence known in this way, having an almost childish glee in affecting abrupt and noisy arrivals. At the same time I was aware of a chilling current of air sweeping through the room that turned the back of my neck to ice. Next, a luminous glow made itself apparent in the corner of the room which my eyes, by this time more used to the darkness, calculated to be opposite that in which the medium was situated inside her fastened cabinet. This was a most solemn moment. Pausing only to offer up a rapid but most fervent prayer of mingled hope and gratitude, I rose from my seat, breaking loose from the restraining hands of my kind neighbours, for the shape that now revealed itself inside the soft luminous glow was that of a little child in her nightgown: it was none other than Rosalie! Oh Mamma, how shall I describe to you the terror and joy of that moment! There she stood, my little darling, gazing eagerly in my direction, as though searching for me, her curls tumbling about her neck and her little hands clasped in an attitude of prayer. For a moment I stood still, straining all my attention towards her, oblivious to anything other than that my beloved child was once more near me, and then the hands tugging at my dress forced me to resume my chair, and Mrs Milk's voice was whispering urgently in my ear that I must not attempt to approach too closely to the apparition lest I violate the vibrations surrounding her and cause harm to the medium entranced inside her bonds.

Murmurs and sobs now arose from all around me as all were struck by this proof of God's most exquisite compassion and mercy. To be precise, as I must strive to be, it was the ladies who sobbed out loud; the gentlemen proved their superior moral strength by remaining silent, sober, calm. Yet William's hand, newly clasping mine as I sank back towards him, was, I swear, wet with the manly tear he had dashed from his eye. How I loved my husband in that moment for this quiet display of feeling! How ardently I pressed his fingers in return!

Mamma, my darling looked at me and smiled. On her head she wore a little wreath of white roses, exactly as when she lay in her tiny coffin at rest, and in her hand she carried a bunch of the selfsame flowers. My soul yearned towards her with all the passion of which it was capable; my eyes drank her in. After that initial desire to start forwards and press her, enclosed in my hungry maternal arms, to my heart, I was content to be allowed simply to *see* her, exactly as I remembered her, to delight, as of old, in the merry countenance overspread with smiles, the eyes so full of trust and love, the little red lips that moved in soundless affectionate lisping. Oh! To be near her was to be in Heaven myself. To be reunited with her at that moment was to experience that sordid and dingy basement transformed into the garden of paradise.

The luminous glow dimmed. The vision faded. My darling vanished, but not before she had blown me a kiss with a playful wave of her little hand.

Behind me, the two worthy female neighbours of Mrs Milk were still weeping, their generous maternal hearts in tune with mine, their own sorrow mitigated by my joy. My soul too full for polite speeches, I turned to them and blessed them. Most heartily I saluted them for that divine feeling which unites women's hearts across the barriers of class and creed! Most readily my tears overflowed afresh and mixed with theirs! Truly, at that moment I experienced what it was to be united in brotherhood with all men before God!

After this climax, the whole company paused. We sought to compose ourselves. Then the voice of Mr Hadbury made itself heard, steadily uplifted in a prayer of thanksgiving, to which we all assented, at its conclusion, with a most readily given amen.

The gas must now be relit and the medium released. This necessitated a little movement, some scraping of chairs, some shuffling. When the light went up, I found that William, with Mr Hadbury and Mr Young, was eagerly examining the ground in front of the cabinet, and that Mrs Milk had remained in her place next to me and was most earnestly enquiring of me how I did. Grateful for her solicitude, I yet shrank from her a little, for her face, so *very* red and coarse, was advanced rather too close to my own. Perceiving this, she removed herself to a little distance, but repeated her enquiries after my health and offered to fetch me a glass of water. I declined this, of course; my spirits were equal to the emergency through which I had just passed; I discovered, as I have said above, that firmness and strength had already been restored to me. No need for cordials, for sedatives, for glasses of water! I assured my worthy hostess, and I spoke the truth, that I needed nothing but the opportunity to thank God at length for the grace so bounteously bestowed on me through the medium of little Flora.

Her attention recalled to her daughter, the mother joined the gentlemen at the door of the cabinet. A minute examination of the flour sprinkled there formerly proved it to have been completely undisturbed, except for one single imprint: that of a tiny foot. We all drew near, to gaze at this in some astonishment. Then Mrs Milk, recollecting herself, begged that we would allow her daughter to be unloosed after what was, she explained, invariably an exhausting ordeal. And so, the cabinet door having been unlocked and swung open, the figure of little Flora was disclosed, still slumped in her swoonlike trance. Once the knots and ropes restraining her had been duly inspected once more, and the seals on them pronounced unbroken, it was the turn of

Mrs Milk to demonstrate her own maternal tenderness, untying her daughter's bonds with her own hands and assisting her to rise and pass into the adjoining room. Nor did I set eyes on Flora again that night: after a seance she is always indisposed and in need of rest and solitude.

I will not trouble you, dearest Mamma, with the details of the rest of that night. Suffice it to say that we returned home and said our prayers of heartfelt gratitude together before I withdrew to my room. I slept deeply, a refreshed and refreshing slumber such as I have not experienced for months stealing upon me as soon as my head touched the pillow. And this morning, although a little agitated as I relive the mingled joy and anguish of that blessed hour, yet I feel myself to be in excellent health, my spirits elastic and my soul beaming and tranquil. Now little William and Henrietta are calling me; I must not neglect *them* in my renewed happiness.

I remain, dearest Mamma, ever your loving daughter,
    Minny.

Ordinary children are born in an ordinary way, crawling in blood and suffering down the birth canal of a woman. I am not ordinary: I was born of the god.

It was the great Father who gave birth to me in the beginning. And during my infancy it is my father who carries me close to his heart, who bears me on his lap, who nurses me on the milk of his wisdom, who nourishes me with his great learning, the power of his words.

I do not need a mother, for I have my father. The ways of women are stupid and frivolous; I scorn them. I am not a woman like other women, gossiping in corners of their trivial obsessions, messing with make-up and finery. I am my father's daughter. I am good as a boy. I have disciplined my body to stay slender and firm and swift; I have disciplined my mind likewise. I speak with men; I speak as men do; I speak of men's things. I am better than other women, for I am both beautiful and wise, both clever and courageous, both understanding and powerful. I walk in my father's way, the only way I wish to know, the one true way.

How could it be otherwise? For my destiny is to follow my father and one day to become as powerful as he.

My father has often told me the story of my birth. How he and his queen, the woman some call my mother but I do not, were seated one day in one of the courts of the palace, and how the great god Amun suddenly made himself visible before them, to the wonder and terror of all. Amun caused my mother to rise, then seat herself beside him on a couch of gold. At the same time my soul was being fashioned on a potter's wheel by other gods. When the pregnant queen gave birth on the royal birth-chair, she was attended by many deities, who ensured that she suffered no pain at all. Thus both my conception and my arrival in the world were the work of the Father of all gods. It was my Father in his divine form who begot and birthed me; his earthly queen being merely the vessel for his power. It is my father through whom I live now and through whom I shall have eternal life.

Dark blue shadows of chimney pots on the tilted grey roofs, a cold and radiant blue sky, sun burnishing the iron railings and the trees. Weather that would normally tug me out to stroll along the canal or in the cemetery that serves our neighbourhood as park; these are not days for staying indoors doing decorating. But I prefer to stick at the slow transformation of the house, watching the past change into the future as I advance through these rooms with brushes and paint. The house as it formerly was lurks just underneath these new glistening surfaces: I see the new house we are gradually creating take shape and colour around us, and I see what should be the old, invisible house still stand strongly behind it, an insistent memory that will keep breaking through. The house has had a skin graft, the clean membrane we've stretched over some of its walls, but we've removed nothing from it that really matters. You don't alter a hundred and thirty years of history with fresh coats of plaster and paint. You can't shut a house up by papering over its gaps; the house has many mouths and keeps talking to me.

Yesterday I finished the bathroom. I cut lengths of lining paper, loaded my brush with paste, worked it to and fro until each long sheet was well coated, floppy and damp, then lifted the thick strips and carried them one by one into the bathroom. The house stuck itself to the lining paper; I stood inside a paper box, a paper bathroom smelling of strong sweet glue. Now the walls were uniformly smooth and white, all bumps and ridges blanked out by the heavy paper. The lavatory cistern, the Ascot, the light fitting, all broke through; I cut round them carefully with my stanley knife. At first they were simply absences in a paper shape; then they acquired three dimensions and the paper fitted itself around them. The paper being so thick made the walls seem warm and soft; I didn't want to paint them after that. I knew I must, so I sploshed on a coat of cream emulsion and painted the plumbing dark blue.

By now it was late afternoon, and I was tired. A bath, I was thinking, with perfumed oil, and a book, then a collapse on the sofa with a glass of wine. When the phone rang I cursed. It was the same old man as last week and the week before, convinced he'd got the right number. I lost my temper with him and slammed the phone down. I went down to the basement to stick my brush in a jar of turps and to fetch up some coal. My head was full of what to cook for supper: pasta with broccoli and anchovies, tomato salad. The light bulb on the stairs had gone. I felt my way down their steepness in the dark, my feet curling over the edge of each tread, my hand gripping the banister. A line of gold showed under the door at the bottom. I was only mildly surprised, assuming you or I had left the light on last night. I cursed gently at the waste of electricity.

At first the door would not budge. Then my fingers remembered to search for the wooden latch, and it suddenly lurched open.

I know the basement as a damp and dirty place that we use for storage and as a carpentry workshop. It's not high on our list of priorities for decoration; we've knocked down the wall separating what were two little rooms to maximize the light from the high barred windows, swept the rubbish of boxes and broken bits into a corner, and left it at that. There was a kitchen here once; the shabby range still stands in the centre of one wall below the chimney breast, thick with dust and cobwebs, there's an ancient deal table and dresser, and a triangular oak cupboard built into the angle of one corner. I keep meaning to come down here and clear up, but I never get round to it; the spiders and woodlice live on undisturbed.

Now the basement appeared to me clean and brightly lit. Sunshine streamed down from the two high windows as though it were mid-morning; a fire burned in the range, which shone with blackleading, the red flames reflected in the copper sauce-pans hanging up nearby. The floor was damp from ancient scrubbing, the brass handles of the dresser and cupboard were a bright tinny yellow, the shallow porcelain sink was white, uncracked.

She was young, and she wasn't looking at me. She didn't seem to have heard me clump down the stairs and come in. She was humming to herself, some skipping rhyme it sounded like.

She stood in the middle of the room, bending over the old deal table on which I keep my paint pots and brushes. All that clutter had gone. A plush cloth, edged with a silky fringe, was draped over the table, and some sort of game or cards were scattered across it. She was arranging the cards in a large circle; I could see that they had letters on them. With one hand she pushed her glossy cardboard oblongs into place; with the other she swept back the long fair hair that fell over her face. Her fingers were blunt and reddened, but deft; they moved across the tablecloth lightly; skilled fingers. She wore a black velvet dress, made high at the throat and tight at the waist, with its thick folds gathered at the back to give a bustle effect. As I watched her, she hopped back to survey the arrangement she had made, gave a little pleased nod. Then she ran over to the dresser, got down a tumbler, and set it in the middle of her circle of cards, upside down. Next she placed her hands palm down on the table, pushed hard several times. The table did not move; it stood solid, four square. Another little nod. She straightened up, putting both hands to her mane of frizzy fair hair and twisting it absentmind-edly at the back of her neck. She had a small, pale face, with a neat curved mouth, a straight little nose, surprisingly dark brows and lashes. Her eyes were large, blue, widely spaced. They glittered like light on water. She could have been fifteen or twenty; her body in the tightly fitting dress was that of a woman, though the way she moved, darting and agile, made her seem a child. I was so interested by her that I moved forwards to see her better.

I broke her self-absorption; she stopped humming, looked up, saw me. Into her face rushed an expression of mingled pleasure and fear. Her hands clasped each other; her eyes opened even wider.

– It's *you*, she stammered: it's *you*.

Still with her eyes fixed on mine, she made me a funny little bow. Now a smile spread over her pale face, and she threw her arms wide in welcome.

I didn't know what to do. How could she possibly know me? I looked down at myself for reassurance. I was wearing my usual decorating gear: a suit of your baggy white painting overalls, big and loose, the legs in deep folds about my feet and the sleeves rolled up to the elbow, a white rag twisted turban-like about my hair to keep it free of paint, an old leather belt around my waist, grubby white trainers.

– Hattie, she breathed: you've come to me again!

Hearing her utter my name was a shock, fear heaving inside me for the first time. I could smell my sweat, sour and cold. I whipped round and pressed the light switch beside the door. As she cried out, the room plunged itself into blackness. When I flicked the switch down again and the light came back on the basement was as I have always known it, chill and dank, thick with dirty spiders' webs and dust. The litter of my painting equipment stood on the dull wood of the tabletop. The fair-haired girl had vanished.

I forced myself to fill the coal-scuttle before slamming the door behind me and groping my way back upstairs. I built and lit the fire in here and crouched next to it to get warm. I wanted whisky inside me. I wanted you to come home and laugh at me, I wanted to hold onto you. Once I stopped shivering I started to write it all down here. To reason myself out of thinking I saw her, out of remembering that she used my name. A pregnant woman's odd fancy, I told myself. My desire for a daughter getting the better of me. But I've written her down as though she's a real ghost.

You have asked me, dear Mr Redburn, for precise details as to why Flora should not be regarded as a *bona fide* medium. Much as it grieves me to strip away the veil from your favourite, sir, and grieves *you* by showing her in her true colours, yet I will do so. A seeker after the truth like yourself deserves no less.

Not so very long ago, I am afraid to say, she was caught out stooping to trickery during the course of a private seance, when she was sitting in the kitchen, as usual, for a circle of neighbours and local friends. A gentleman from Hampstead, a Mr Andrews, who attended, unbeknownst to Flora, as a guest of the officers of the Dalston Spiritualists Association, was present also, and he is able to confirm what I say.

During the course of the seance, Mr Andrews got up from his chair and went towards the corner cabinet, inside which Flora was supposedly securely bound in her chair, in order to witness for himself, at close quarters, the marvels Flora had promised to produce. You remember, I dare say, the luminous spirit face that presents itself floating about in the region of the upper part of the door? We saw it together, the last time you were in London, did we not? Mr Andrews was close enough to see that under its deathly whiteness it bore a striking resemblance to Flora's own. When a white 'spirit' arm was extended, he decided to put his doubts to the test. He grasped the spirit's arm in his own, and felt up along it until he came into contact with a gauze sleeve. This began to shake vigorously. He shouted out at once, for the hand and arm were not cool and spiritual at all, but all too warm and fleshly. He called out for lights, for he had no doubt whatsoever that the spirit arm was in fact firmly attached to Flora's body, for he had felt up as far as her bosom through the wide sleeve, and was sure that Flora had somehow got out of the cabinet.

Despite the commotion that followed, with Flora crying out and the other members of the audience stumbling up in the darkness to see what was the matter, he held on to the hand until he was pushed out of the way by persons he could not identify, the lights still being out, so that he was jostled to one side. Further investigation was then impossible. After five minutes or so, when the gas was lit again, Flora was discovered, dishevelled and breathing heavily, back inside the cabinet, with the ropes that had bound her hands twisted loosely around them and the knots gone.

Well, sir, those that were present who wished to go on believing in Flora's powers will doubtless do so, but Mr Andrews is in no doubt of what happened. He left the house looking very grave. I heard him mutter what sounded like: *Potson*. That, as you must know, sir, is the name of a once-famous medium recently exposed for trickery.

Sir, it makes me wretched to be the cause of your unhappiness. Flora has been your protégée for so long, it must cut you to the heart to know that she has been exposed in such shameful and ungenerous tricks. Please do not think the worse of me for bringing them to your notice. I am grieved myself, for the enemies of spiritualism are keen and crafty, and Flora has set the whole movement back by what she has done. All real mediums must feel, as I do, that she has cast doubt on the practice of those who act in good faith for the advancement of knowledge. This wound to the movement will not easily be healed. Nor, I know, will the wound to your affectionate heart.

I continue to rely on you, sir, for the reasons I gave in my last, to be utterly discreet as to the source of this information, which I have laid with you only after much heart-searching. But in any case, you do not need to rely on my word alone. Mr Andrews, I believe, intends to publish an account of the wickedness he witnessed.

I remain, dear Mr Redburn, your sincere wellwisher and little friend.

Rosina unwillingly helps me get ready. I've threatened to tell Mother about George if she doesn't. An important occasion. I wash myself all over, wash my hair too: when it's wet it's easier to curl. Clean underclothes; my one good set in linen without any darns. Rosina laces me up tight to show off my neat pretty waist, lends me her best pair of stockings, the silk ones, and her coral bracelet. I want to look as young as possible, so I don't put my hair up: I just fluff it out with my fingers so that the curls settle right and let it flow over my shoulders and down my back. There's not much we can do with my black velvet; it's shabby and rubbed, but Rosie gives it a good brush while I dab blacking onto my Sunday boots. A puff of mother's violet scent spray behind my ears and on my throat. Cut-glass bottle; rubber bulb covered in crocheted lavender silk. My one pair of gloves is much-washed and much-mended but it can't be helped. I chew a cachou just to make sure my breath is sweet; Rosina says ladies never eat onions but I don't care. She holds the little looking glass for me, moving it up and down so that I can see myself in bits: neck, mouth, elbow, ear. I'll do. My stomach heaves; I breathe deeply, willing myself to calm down. Rosie gives me the thumbs-up, then I'm creeping downstairs into the hall and making for the front door. I've told Mother we're going to one of Mr Hadbury's lectures on psychical science, but I don't want her to catch me looking so smart; she'd demand to know what's up.

Round the corner, in Montgomery Villas, we part, me to make for the hackney carriage stand a hundred yards further on and Rosina to stroll towards the canal bridge where she's promised to meet George. Something Mother would be horrified by. She thinks Rosie much too young to be walking out.

The maid's black dress is finer than mine. Her eyes scratch me, then she announces that Lady Preston is not at home. I know that, of course; I wouldn't be here otherwise. I sigh, cast my eyes down in disappointment, then ask for Sir William. After a moment's frown she lets me in to a large hall floored in black and white marble. I want to pause, gawp at the mirrors and stands of greenery and the tall elegant clock, but she opens another door and pushes me inside, snapping that she'll go and see whether her master's at home. Her name is Wilson; later on we become quite good friends. She suffers from Minny Preston, in her way, as much as I do in mine.

This must be the library: a thick crimson carpet under my feet, scarlet and jade-green flowers on the wallpaper, what you can see of it between all the pictures. Tall open cupboards full of books in browny-gold calf bindings. A circular table in the centre of the room is heaped with periodicals and magazines. There are comfortable-looking low chairs with embroidered cushions, a big sofa, a large fire crackling redly in the white marble fireplace, a small table covered with pots of ferns and ivies. It's the prettiest room I've ever been in; nor have I ever seen so many books in one place. They draw me to them irresistibly. How my father would have loved this room! I'm hungrily looking and touching and opening one gold-tooled volume after another when I hear the door open and close and spin round to find him there watching me.

I can see from his face that he's not angry, so I don't apologize, just blush and look shyly at him.

– So you're a reader, are you, Miss Milk? he enquires: in addition to your other talents?

He moves towards me, taking his time. What a handsome man!

Tall and vigorous; in his prime; thick dark brown hair and beard; full red lips; deep-set eyes under thick brows. When I met him for the first time, at the meeting in Dalston, he looked serious, even grim. Today he's smiling. And everything about him is so well-kept and clean: his fingernails, his shirt, his boots. I start to feel very heavy, as though I'm shrinking. My weight will pull me down. I'm short, I'm grubby, I'm badly dressed. I think he guesses how I'm feeling: he takes my hand in his for a moment, then leads me to the fire and settles me in a chair and asks very kindly what he can do for me.

This is the moment. I have a whole speech prepared. One that I've practised in front of the mirror, in front of Rosie. But, looking at him, I can see the speech won't work; too pat. So I abandon it, clasp my hands together in my lap, lean forwards with my eyes fixed on his and blurt out a few garbled sentences.

He raises a hand. Beautiful long fingers he has, with a signet ring on the littlest one.

– My dear Miss Milk. Don't, I beg you, agitate yourself. Please. Take your time. I'm at your disposal. Now then.

His smile and his courtesy calm me down. I blow my nose then start again. Haltingly I describe my distress over Mr Redburn's accusations that I'm a trickster, all the nasty slanders he has begun spreading about me in his letters to *The Spiritualist Magazine*, the article in *The Times* that quotes his views and backs them up.

– They're false, sir, I sob: but who's to believe me if Mr Redburn says not to? You know his power and influence in the spiritualist world as well as I do. If he says I'm a charlatan then I'm done for.

– My dear child, he murmurs: my dear child.

– I'll lose everything, I go on: my good name, my reputation. I'll be a laughing-stock at best, and at worst a criminal. I'm ruined.

By now I'm crying so hard I don't see or hear him get up. The lightest of touches on my hair. I catch my breath, open my eyes. He wheels off, walks up and down between the big long windows with their view over the square then returns towards me and leans against the mantelpiece, looking down at me. I gaze back at him, hoping my face isn't too red and tearstained. Rosina always looks like a pig after *she's* been crying.

– My dear Miss Milk, he says: I do, believe me, understand your distress, and sympathize with it. But I'm at a loss to know how I can help you, much as I might wish to.

61

I give a little sob.

– Oh sir. It's been so good of you to listen. I hardly dare go on. But *you*, sir, will forgive me if I seem to be impertinent.

He smiles.

– Be courageous, Miss Milk. Continue.

– It's just that, I burst out: you've witnessed several of my seances. You've seen a little of what I can do. You saw the table lift itself and move around, and the chair on which I was sitting go up and down?

He nods.

– Well, sir, I go on: you're not just a layman, like Mr Redburn. You're a professor. A scientist. You're famous for the work you do in physics. Everybody knows about your researches into Mr Home's mediumship. If you, sir, were to vouch for me, if you were to write to *The Spiritualist Magazine* to declare that you believe me to be as genuine a medium as Mr Home, then I should be in the clear.

I gaze at him as beseechingly as I know how.

Another of those slow smiles of his.

– But, my dear Miss Milk. Fascinated as I have been by your performances in Dalston, which I shall certainly never forget, it is one thing for me to declare to you now, in private, how much I am impressed by the phenomena you produced, but quite another for me to proclaim in public that I am totally convinced by your powers! The scientific community, you know, does not work in quite that way. My simple word is not enough in this case.

– Oh I know, sir, I break in: there must be proof, there must be experiments, there must be tests. I know all this. But could *you*, sir, not make them?

I stand up and face him. I have rehearsed this next part several times.

– I am ready, sir, I declare: to submit myself to the severest scrutiny science can provide! I am ready to make myself available to the penetrating gaze of one such as yourself who can *not* be tricked! I am ready to be examined under any conditions stipulated by my examiner! I am ready to face the most probing of questions! I will do anything to prove to you and to the public that I am not involved in any trickery, and that my mediumship is real!

He takes my hand.

– Miss Milk, I am much moved by what you say. By your sincerity. Speaking as someone old enough to be your father, I must say that I certainly should not like either of my daughters to be in your predicament. Undoubtedly you have suffered much from the aspersions cast upon your good faith.

I stay silent and just go on looking at the top button of his waistcoat, standing still while his eyes flicker over my mouth, my throat, my breast.

– Your case interests me strangely, he pursues: and it is true that, having terminated my researches on Mr Home, I have not exhausted my interest in the subject of spiritualism. There remain, I am convinced, fresh fields to be explored, new territories to be opened up.

I let my fingers move in his. An almost imperceptible pressure. I let the power of my wanting flow from me, down into my palm, and so into his. I like his touch; it is warm and dry.

– Sir, I venture: I could show you now, if you have the time, some more of the things I am capable of. I could prove to you here in this room the depth of my sincerity. You would not regret it, sir, I am sure of that.

We pause. I am trembling, and I know he can feel it: he holds my excitement as he holds my hand.

– Very well, Miss Milk, he murmurs finally: I shall give orders that I am not to be disturbed for the next hour, and during that time I shall put your powers to the test. It is up to you to convince me that it will be worth my while to examine your capabilities further and to furnish you with the testimonial you seek.

– Oh sir, I tell him: you will not be disappointed. I can promise you that. You are giving me the chance I so desperately need, and I am very grateful. I will not let you down!

He releases my hand. My mouth is suddenly dry. I run my tongue over my lips, to moisten them.

– Have you all that you need? he enquires: is the room sufficiently dark? Are you warm enough?

He pulls the curtains, then goes out of the room to speak to the servant. I lie down on the sofa, settling a pink silk cushion under my head, then clasping my hands loosely together in my lap. I breathe deeply in and out, letting my mind go blank, letting it open up to whatever may choose to come to me out of the warm darkness. I am growing drowsy, yet at the same time my mind is perfectly clear. I am open, and I am empty.

A click, as he closes the library door. I don't know how many seconds pass before he is seating himself on a low chair next to the sofa. I shut my eyes.

– Now, sir, I whisper: I am ready.

Once again, dearest Mamma, I take up my pen to write to you after far too long an interval. Be not alarmed that you have not heard from me for several weeks, however; my health continues good, though I can no longer get about as much as I should like, and the children and William are likewise very well. The date of my confinement approaching so near, Dr Felton considers it advisable that I should rest as much as possible, in order to conserve my strength, for you know what I always suffer at that time, and I have been, of course, grateful for his advice. Yet I will confess to you that these evening hours of solitary repose and inactivity, following upon days uninterrupted by the many household duties I was formerly accustomed to perform when not in my present delicate situation, are conducive, if I am not very severe upon myself, to a certain melancholy. I have time to *think*, and I find myself reflecting both upon the past and the present with no little degree, sometimes, of apprehension.

Oh Mamma: supposing I should die when my time comes to be delivered? Who will look after my dear little children then? Poor little motherless creatures: what will become of them? And my own William: how will he manage alone, bereft of his helpmeet? These are morbid fancies, I know, and indeed I endeavour to check them as far as I may, and as the doctor says I must, yet it is impossible to banish them totally from my mind. Death stalks me. I have seen his face before this. I tremble at his power. I have resigned myself to it before now!

If it were not for little Flora's presence in our midst I do not know what I should do! But I must recollect: you do not know, of course, of the recent addition to our household. My dear protégée has at long last been prevailed upon, along with her sister, Miss Rosina Milk, to pay us a visit. That, of course, is a source of the utmost satisfaction to me, for it is several weeks now since I have cherished the hope of being of some real practical help to her.

It came about like this. You will remember I told you of my concern, once William had described her situation to me, that

Flora's gifts exposed her, if she were to give them the full expression that we are all sure God's loving will demands, to the excited scrutiny of the multitude, to the vulgar speculations of a public drawn more by idle curiosity than by true reverence, to contact with unscrupulous persons only too ready to be in close proximity to a young, beautiful and innocent girl. Vice walks those eastern streets; I know it; how many young women of Flora's class have fallen prey to his seductions! Vice walks those streets in *female* form; I know this too, from the guarded words my dear husband has occasionally let fall (his medical training at the hospital, as you know, brought him daily into contact with the lowest degrees of human degradation and misery); heaven forfend that my Flora should ever fall prey to the machinations of some evil woman and be drawn into such a life, whose only end is foul disease and lingering wretched death!

Forgive me, Mamma, for mentioning these terrible subjects. Yet, in my capacity as Flora's affectionate patroness, I have been forced to dwell upon them, not least because the dark angel of temptation has already brushed Flora's shoulder with his wing. My darling is innocent, of course, I hasten to add; but it is that very innocence of hers, which, while it enables her to walk unscathed through the fiery furnaces of public appearances as a medium, yet opens her to possible danger. I refer not only to the fact that the meetings of the Dalston Spiritualists Association are held in the upstairs room of a large public house frequented, apparently, by unaccompanied women of most uncertain reputation, but to something else so horrid I shudder to describe it.

I visited Flora last week. Alone, this time, our intimacy being such by now that I was happy, on this occasion, to dispense with my dear husband's escort, he being, in any case, occupied at his laboratory. He agreed with me that there could be no harm in my travelling there in a cab with the blinds well pulled down and with my thickest veil and cloak to protect my interesting condition from public view. I found Flora, as usual, in the little parlour where she is used to spend what few hours of leisure she has being obliged to occupy herself with the family's mending and darning and I know not what. There being no servant to let me in (some great coarse girl comes in to help Mrs Milk with the weekly washing and scrubbing, but I have never laid eyes on her, I am not sorry to say) Flora received me herself, and I could not help observing, as she showed me into a seat by the fire (her family, though apparently struggling to maintain a decent standard of living, does not scruple to have *large fires* constantly burning) how at the same time she hastily threw a shawl over a large basket of intimate woollen garments of the most shabby looking sort. Poor Flora! She was made to live in a purer sphere! Such, as I saluted her with an earnest and friendly kiss, was the content of the ejaculation that first sprang to my lips. Fearing I had offended her, for she moved away from me, her eyes suddenly full of tears, I sat in silence for a few moments, while she seated herself opposite me and struggled to regain her composure. At length I ventured to remark that there was surely something the matter, more than the usual dejection consequent upon the dreary daily performance of her routine household tasks, and I begged her to tell me what it was.

After a little prompting on my part, she overcame her reluctance. Indeed, she has no secrets from me. It was my friendly persuasion a little while ago that first encouraged her to admit how it oppresses her to be forced to spend so much time cooking and sewing rather than quietly reading and meditating as her soul craves, and it was my sympathy, on that occasion, that enabled her to go on to express her wish to help her family, in the sense of paying for a servant to take over more of the domestic drudgery, by performing at as many seances in public as she was able. A medium, I was astonished to learn, can command *substantial* fees from such public work. I remonstrated at first, so shocked was I that God's work should be mingled with any consideration of financial reward, but in the end I was obliged to accept the fact, and to tolerate the idea that a young girl with such elevated spiritual gifts as Flora's should actually be forced to accept remuneration for them. People of *that* class, I was forced to conclude, must dispense with many of the ideals that motivate *us*. And it did Flora no final disservice in my eyes to recognize that she is keenly aware both of her responsibilities towards her family and of her membership of a different social milieu to my own. She never presumes, delicate and refined as her sensibilities so surprisingly are, to suppose that we are equal: her attitude towards me is governed by the warmest gratitude and respect. It is this knowledge of hers of the barrier between us, of course, that excites my wish to help her. She is so unfortunate as to have the *aspirations*, if not the *capacities*, of a lady. I never snub her on this point; I always talk to her as gently as I can on this subject, for it is impossible not to be moved by the ardent longings for a better life that have been awakened in her as a result of public recognition of her great gifts.

It was this, indeed, that she wished to discuss with me on this occasion. Very pretty it was, to see her overcome at last the shame and diffidence forbidding her to confide her difficulty! A difficulty that no young woman, in my opinion, should *ever* be forced to confront. Flora, once I had clasped her hands in mine and assured her of my sympathy, poured out her heart in the most touching way, pausing every now and again to let a maidenly blush ebb from her cheek, to wipe a sparkling tear from her downcast eye. What she had to tell me was shocking enough. The gentleman who has been so good as regularly to assist her family (Mr Charles Redburn, a native of Yorkshire and the owner of a large manufacturing concern near Halifax) has begun, in his letters, to hint at subjects of a most indelicate and improper nature, in fact to suggest that in return for his financial gifts Flora should consent to live under his protection!

I was not a little astonished, firstly that Flora's fame had travelled so far beyond London (another effect, I fear, of those public appearances whose necessity I so deprecate), and secondly, that her fortunes were so closely tied up with the whimsical generosity of a comparative stranger so much older than herself. Most solemnly she assured me of his initially purely paternal benevolence, his hitherto disinterested regard for her welfare, his originally keen devotion to the mysteries of her craft and his equally keen appreciation of the spiritual benefits therefrom accruing. Still, I could not quite like it that my young friend could ever have put herself to such an extent in his power, could ever have become to such an extent dependent on him, for look where this has led. I ventured to suggest that it was perhaps part of the plan of Providence that Flora should immediately detach herself from him. She replied, weeping, that that was all very well, but what would become of her now?

She rose at this point from where she had been kneeling at my feet, her head in my lap, and fetched a packet of letters from the bureau in the corner. These, she said, were Mr Redburn's earliest communications to her. They were indeed avuncular, they breathed a spirit of Christian warmth and concern that could only disgust me when I thought of what came after, and they were written in a style that was blunt to the point of vulgarity.

No good, I remained convinced, could ever have come from Flora's association with such a patron. That her withdrawal might occasion her *financial* distress I could well see, since it threw her back on the necessity of increasing the public perform- ances that she has learned to dread from the time I pointed out to her the evils they exposed her to.

How my heart bled for the poor unfortunate child! I took her back into my arms and enquired of her why she had not approached William for advice before this, given the respect he commands as a well-known and brilliant professor of science, and the interest with which the scientific community awaits the outcome of his present researches into psychic phenomena? She replied, through her sobs, that she would not so far presume as to dare to approach the great Sir William Preston for help, for, infinitely sensible as she was of his kindness in showing his interest in her work to the degree that he had already done, it would indeed be wicked of her to expect, or ask for, anything more. Nor was her dilemma one she could possibly mention to a gentleman. No, what she had need of, and here she wept afresh, was the sympathy and consolation that only a woman friend, in this case myself, could provide.

I was struck afresh by this additional proof of her innate delicacy and refinement (one which, I flatter myself, I have had no little part in eliciting and in encouraging to bloom), but felt obliged to hide my emotion and to enquire of her what her mother proposed to do about the present distressing situation? For I remained keenly aware, of course, that hers must be the final judgment, hers the final arbitration. Now my poor Flora recounted to me her mother's anguish on the occasion of her daughter's reputation being threatened, her total ignorance of how to obtain redress, her unwillingness to risk further damage by writing to Mr Redburn herself to defend her child.

I cannot tell you what outrage this account of Mr Redburn's vile behaviour produced in my breast, and what a resolution to defend my little friend sprang up in me as I watched her try to check her tears, nay, even to smile. How lovely she looked at that moment in the black velvet dress she always wears (the only one of any quality, I believe, that she *possesses*), with her pale face bearing only too obviously the marks of her recent inward suffering, yet with that light shining in her eyes that would *not* be quenched! At that moment, such was the nobility of soul that streamed from her countenance and bearing, I felt that we were truly sisters, and told her so, pressing her to me once more and assuring her that I would do everything in my power to help her. For answer, she seized my hand and laid it against her lips.

I asked her whether we should not now ask for help and inspiration from God, whether we should not now hold a seance, just the two of us, in order to make contact with Flora's friendly guides in the Great Beyond and submit ourselves to their wisdom and advice? I will confess to you that my question was not wholly disinterested, it being two weeks since I had attended the seance which I described in my last letter, two weeks since I had tasted the joy of seeing my little Rosalie again, and two weeks since that cup had been snatched from me!

Flora looked mournful, however, at my suggestion, and regretfully shook her head. It was impossible, she explained, in her present agitated state, which clouded and spoiled the vibrations from the spirit world, to enter the necessary trance. This could not be forced; it was a gift offered by the spirits themselves, and they never approached her when she was embroiled in too much earthly distress. The medium, she stressed, was a vessel, and the vessel must be clear and unmuddied, unsullied by personal grief, however much she felt for the sorrows of those she attempted to serve. Let her once survive this terrible and lonely time of trial, and she would once more be restored, she was sure, to a full enjoyment of her former capacities.

This was a blow to me indeed. I took my leave of her in a very subdued mood, pausing only to reiterate my promise of support, and returned home.

That evening, after dinner, when William retired as is his wont when he is at home, to his study, I rose and followed him there. I scrupled not to open my whole heart to him; I laid Flora's dilemma before him; I pleaded with all the gentle wifely force of which I was capable for the urgency of aiding her, and rescuing her from temptation. He was as appalled and astonished, when he heard all, as I had been, and asked me what I thought we should do, in what way we could assist my young friend? For he understood and applauded the cogency of my reasoning that since we had witnessed the phenomena that were being halted by forces of evil outside Flora's control we had a moral obligation to step forward. My dear husband, never one to undervalue his wife, always ready to listen to the deepest stirrings of her heart, bent his head towards me and silently encouraged me to go on. *Then* I told him my plan. *Then* he praised my daring. *Then* he acknowledged me as noble and generous indeed amongst my sex!

In short, Flora is come to stay with us, for an indefinite period, and her presence here is, as I said at the very beginning of this letter (which I fear, dearest Mamma, to be wearyingly long for your perusal) a source of great joy and comfort to me. She is somewhere about the house at present with Charles and Ralph. She plays with them so charmingly! We foretold, you see, that with her sturdy independence she would not wish to be beholden to us for her bed and board, and it has turned out just as we thought. In the morning she keeps the younger children occupied while Nurse is busy with other duties, and in the afternoons she does a little light sewing for me or reads to me, depending on how I am feeling. Her sister Miss Rosina has accompanied her, as I said before, and they share a sweet little bedroom up in the attic. How relieved I am that my Flora no longer has to submit herself to the cruel gaze of the Hackney public! It is a source of great contentment to me that she has so readily submitted to my superior judgment on this matter, and that she has been so unfailingly grateful to be relieved of having to take such a heavy responsibility for helping to support her family: William, with his eternal generosity, has undertaken to pay them a weekly stipend during the period of her residence with us.

So: I have gained a loving and a faithful companion (and indeed Miss Rosina Milk too is a young woman of no small intelligence and attraction) as well as the services of an ardent and capable medium. Of our seances together I will tell you much more in my next letter.

Now, fearing to exhaust your motherly patience by the excessive length of this missive, I will content myself with sending you all the love in the world from your daughter,

    Minny.

*

Armed with the knowledge of my miraculous beginnings, I am serene in the face of my second birth: the great test that is my initiation.

I am born into my new life exactly as I shall be joined to the gods when I die. Veiled in black linen, I lie on my bier in the funeral barge, which departs upstream to the wails of mourners, the screech of flutes. My bandaged eyes see nothing. I lie as still as though I have been drugged into slumber, my arms straight down by my sides, my feet together. I am carried ashore, up the sloping covered causeway where no one ever goes except the priests and the kings travelling towards eternal life, and into the mortuary temple. My bier is lowered, then placed on the floor. I hear the bearers and priests depart.

I am utterly alone. I can feel my isolation on my skin, cold and clammy. No sound. No echoes. Nothing stirring except the hairs rising up along my arms, my quick breathing.

I untie my blindfold and sit up.

Blackness surrounds me, thick as dust in my nostrils and mouth. My eyes can't pierce it. Then the curtains of darkness slowly part, and I peer forwards into the gloom.

I am reclining in a forest of stone trees. All I can see are the massive trunks of the stone columns stretching away from me in every direction, their tops invisible. They march in closely packed avenues, exactly aligned, darkness between them. I stretch out my hand and touch cold solidity. Three steps in either direction and I should be lost, never to find my way out. Better to stay still, and to stay here. Better to strain my eyes into the darkness, to follow the stray shafts of bright sunlight cutting down from the high blackness above me and illuminating the edge of a stone base, the sharp detail of a carved hieroglyph. Never have I known such a weight, such an extent, of darkness, of cold, of isolation.

I hear him coming from a long way off: the slow slap of his sandals on the stone floor, the whisper of his robes dragging behind him. Then his breathing, steady and slow. I abandon myself to prayer: I crouch down and wait for him.

I am at the beginning of the world. This temple is the swamp that rises when the river floods go down: the start of creation. Fat belly of rich mud from which burst forth creatures, plants, human beings. Around me, petrified in ardent stone stretching to the heavens, are the palm trees, the lotus flowers in bud, the clumps of papyrus. In front of me is the god.

So that I should not be frightened, he has put on a disguise: he has come to me as Thoth, a gold ibis mask covering his face, his scribal palette slung by a strap from his shoulder, over a cloak of gold feathers fastened by a gold clasp, golden sandals on his feet.

I follow him through the central avenue of the great temple, the stone trees falling away behind us in their orderly and massive rows. Through the high gates we go, under the stone colonnade, until a fourth, smaller hall of columns, deep in the heart of the temple, ends at the entrance to what seems a sanctuary. Here, set into the walls at regular intervals, are niches with stone altars in them, and on one of these stone couches the god causes me to lie down.

The light has been banished. I can see the gleam of the mask, nothing more. When he puts his hands on me I shudder. Not the sharp bird claws I feared, but the gentle fingers of a man.

My father has warned me that whatever happens I must lie still, I must be obedient, must yield myself utterly to the power of the god. Only the courageous pass through this rite and emerge into the light of immortality. I, who have been born once of the god already, must show no fear when the god comes for me again and tests me. I must be worthy of him.

His hands on my shoulders press me down into further darkness. He is the one I worship and have waited for so long. I am ready.

I know his true name. I know whose face is concealed by the harsh jutting beak. It is not fear that courses through me and dissolves my limbs, but anticipation.

This morning I woke up shouting, out of a nightmare. The one that has visited me ever since I was seven years old. Though I've had it only recently since I've been with you; your warm body has almost completely driven it away. Had. Last night it came back: the burglar's sweet stale breath, his wobbly hands, his urgent whispers echoing in the dark, disembodied, like a voice on the telephone. Then there was a violent death I felt inside me, that ripped me up, that shocked me with its force of pain. When I woke up I was shouting, and then so relieved to be awake, to know it was only a dream, that I began to cry. Then I remembered that my baby is dead, and stopped crying.

At the hospital they said that the embryo had hardly formed. Something had gone badly wrong, almost from the beginning. Shreds of flesh, that's all my baby was. My body detonated a time-bomb and killed her.

Part of the dream was a scan. It showed me the miscarriage happening. Like watching the news on a TV screen. Images of war. A city topples, buildings shake and dissolve apart, fall on the living and bury them. Countless children dead under plaster and rubble. My baby is one of them.

In the dream my mother was not there. My absent mother did not reappear to be with me. I blamed her for abandoning me, for not teaching me how to look after things and make sure they did not get broken. In the dream I did not have to blame myself.

My baby, who was alive, is dead. I can't grasp it.

I didn't know she was dead. I thought she was alive. I went on talking to her inside myself, as I've done ever since I knew I was pregnant. For how long was I talking to someone who was no longer there? She was a person, alive and real, with whom I have, with whom I had, a relationship. Then they were scraping the red bits of her out of me. There was no dead body we could bury in the ground and hold a funeral for. There was nothing they would let me touch or see, just a sealed plastic bag, I don't know what colour, that went to the hospital incinerator. The smoke from its chimneys, I read in the local paper yesterday, helps pollute the atmosphere.

I say 'she', but of course I don't know that I had a daughter. I won't call her 'it'. At the hospital they explained that they couldn't tell the sex, there was just this mess inside me. These shreds of dead flesh.

Everyone is very kind to me, including you of course. I am numb. I've had a shock: a baby being dragged out of me in bits. I've given birth. The baby's gone.

None of this means anything. I'm writing it down here just in case it does. I should like to declare that I did have a baby inside me, and that now I don't. That's a fact. Another fact is that she was dead weeks before I knew it, and so I can't trust myself to know anything for sure, nor that I'm able to make babies and keep them alive.

For me the baby's still alive. She's a weight inside me, hard and heavy and very bitter. She hurts.

Tonight, since there are guests for dinner, Rosina and I shall eat downstairs in the kitchen with the housekeeper and the maids to save Cook the trouble of making us a separate meal that has to be brought up to the nursery. I shan't mind exchanging that brown room with its barred windows and scarred inky table for the cheerful company of the kitchen, and nor will Rosina. Minny puts across her order as an apologetic request, clearly thinking we'll mind not being asked to eat in the gloomy dining room smelling of old mutton and potatoes, that it's hard on us not to have the chance of sitting opposite the portrait of her sour-lipped grandfather for two hours without speaking a word. But while Minny's picking her way through some dainty mess in a French sauce we'll be feasting on a nice bit of boiled beef and carrots with Yorkshire pudding, and afterwards, once Rosina's settled to a game of cards with Wilson and the others, I'll be able to slip out all the more easily, up the area steps.

– Tonight, Minny adds: there's no need for you and your sister to join us after dinner in the drawing room. I don't want to overtax your strength.

I'm her pet, captured from the savage wilderness, tamed and trained to perform for the amusement of ladies and gentlemen in evening clothes. Minny can't trust me to prowl neatly among the knives and forks and finger-bowls, though any slips with coffee cups can be forgiven just so long as I make sure to go into trance afterwards. But the spirits aren't to be treated that way. I can't turn Hattie on and off like a tap. She comes to me when *she* chooses: she's queen of a greater country than Bayswater.

Minny's bedroom is much prettier than the cold dark dining room downstairs. No wonder she spends so much time up here. The wallpaper is patterned with forget-me-nots on a white ground, and the carpet is sky colour, scattered with wreaths of pink and yellow roses. Her bed is hung with white muslin curtains spotted with pale blue, looped back with blue silk cords, and its pillows are deeply edged with lace. My eye, cherishing, travels over the blue and gold porcelain ornaments on the marble mantelpiece, the twin silver candlesticks in the shape of twining ivy stems, the oval miniatures framed in crinkly gilt, the inlaid workbox, the fluted vase of pink glass holding a bunch of creamy roses with deeply serrated leaves, the little bookcase crammed with novels and volumes of poetry.

Minny yawns and stretches, arching her little feet in their embroidered slippers, curling her hands into fists, closing her eyes and throwing her head back, parting her lips to show the tip of her pink tongue. Her blue dressing-gown falls open with her movement. The thin robe underneath moulds the swell of her belly, pushing upwards against silk. I judge her to be six months gone at least. She's told me that tonight's dinner party will be the last for some time.

She opens her eyes and catches me watching her. She's shameless, sticking herself out like this. I duck my head, concentrate on pushing my needle through the great rent in little William's frock. I know she can see my discomfort. She enjoys it.

– Flora, she says: wouldn't *you* like to be married and have a baby?

As she speaks, her hand, dangling over the padded arm of her chair, touches the little round table that stands there, that we sometimes use for seances. On it, now, is Minny's collection of miniature boxes. Ivory, silver, cloisonné, mother-of-pearl. Her finger trails over them, lingers, moves on. Her finger is a signpost, pointing towards a mystery: a new box I haven't seen before. I lean forward, to let my own fingers caress the twist of fine gold wire that encircles the enamel lid decorated in pink and green, a design of two butterflies perched on a leaf. Just big enough to keep sweets in, or nibs, or pills. Minny doesn't use her boxes for anything. She just looks at them.

– So pretty, I tell her: who gave it you?

Minny's complexion brightens, a red flush sweeping across her high forehead.

– I've had that one for ages, she snaps: William gave it to me. You've forgotten it, that's all.

She pushes the boxes about on the satiny table top. Now the one with the pink butterflies stands next to a silvery heart-shaped one studded with bits of turquoise. The same colour as the ribbons on Minny's nightgown laid out on her bed, the arms folded neatly across the breast.

She's fiddling with her hair now, smoothing and lifting it, pushing the pins in at new angles.

– You ought to get married, Flora dear, she prattles on: someone as pretty as you should have no trouble. You won't be left single for very long, I feel sure! All the gentlemen admire you so!

She jabs with a hairpin, misses. One heavy lock falls to her lace and silk shoulder. Her belly is swollen and fat, a field that's been rained on, full of greenness, a tight pod ready to pop and spill out its peas.

– I'll never marry, I inform her, biting off another length of thread and steering it towards my needle's eye: I'll never bear children. I don't want to be a wife or a mother.

My poor mother once tried to give herself an abortion. She jumped off the kitchen table, over and over, onto the floor and then back up again, but couldn't dislodge the child inside. She told me this on the way to Father's funeral. She was distraught and didn't know what she was saying, but I know it was the truth. The week after the funeral it was Father's birthday. As I sat at the kitchen table and wept for him the spirits came to me for the first time and made the table leap up and down. The table shook off all its grief, it hopped and danced. That was when I knew I was destined to be a medium. My mother gave in to her pregnancy, and gave birth. She gave birth eight times in all. This will be Minny's tenth lying-in. I've heard my mother's sufferings in labour through the bedroom wall. That terrible tearing pain, over and over and over again. I shouldn't be able to bear it.

– Never marry, my dear Flora? Minny is exclaiming: what can you be thinking of? You're hardly the person to dwindle into an old maid.

Next, my poor mother tried tumblers of gin and water, and a boiling bath that wrinkled her skin into scarlet folds but did not swill out the baby. She resigned herself then; she drew the line at poking herself with knitting needles. She told me all this, blubbing it out, as we jolted to the cemetery with Father's coffin.

There are too many children. There can be too many. You know that, Minny Preston. Just as well as I do. How did little Rosalie die? Tell me *that*. Tell me, too, how much you're longing for this replacement.

– Flora!

Minny's mouth has puckered up as though I've ladled salt into it. Did I speak aloud? I must be more careful. She's pretending to look puzzled, but she's scared: she knows I *know*. And she's terrified I'll tell William what I know.

– I think, she says, leaning back: it is time for me to bathe and dress. Would you be so good, my dear Flora, as to ring for my maid?

On an evening like this one, when the servants are too flustered and busy to bother with us, Rosina and I carry up the cans of water ourselves if we want a bath. No fireplace in our attic. I shudder at the thought of taking off all my clothes to crouch in the tin tub we borrow from Wilson's room next door. I shall make do with a cat's lick and a promise.

Rosina does my hair for me, then I start to brush hers. You have to pull it outwards, hard, away from the scalp. She yowls and puts up one hand to her forehead where the skin is tightly stretched back by the strokes of my brush. I take no notice and carry on. All my life I've had to look after the younger ones; I never could afford to pay too much attention to their complaints. I am determined that Rosina's hair shan't be as frizzy as mine, so I make sure it gets a good brushing every day. I'm severe with her about it.

– Flora, she whimpers: I don't like it here. I want to go home.

I won't have her moan and sulk. I raise the hairbrush to her, only half playfully, and she subsides.

– You can't go home, I tell her: you've got to stay just a little bit longer until the experiments are finished. You know I can't stay here on my own without you.

– I don't like this house, Rosie says.

I understand very well what she means. With less to employ her here than I have, she spends more time alone than I do, up in our attic room, in a silence thick as felt. The ache of boredom; dulled by romances read as drugs. To make time pass quicker. Too much time, dragging its feet and snarling. Time halts, and threatens. I myself find most of the rooms in this house the wrong size, criss-crossed by invisible walls, obstacles preventing my way through. Sounds echo and ping and startle me. I tiptoe across deep soft carpets I might drown in; I peer round the edge of blinds. To be alone in this house is to know an emptiness I can't fill. I creep and scuttle through these too-large rooms. It's different when William comes home; the house pulls itself together and starts to live. But for most of the day the house languishes. An ocean of cold water, with an undertow of anxiety that wraps itself around your ankles like weed and tries to pull you down.

I drop the hairbrush onto the washstand and start to gather up the fat horsetail of hair, a brown plume, in my hands.

– Please, Rosie-Posy. Just give me a little more time.

– I ought to be getting started with the dressmaking, she grumbles: it's not fair, we always have to do what *you* want. What about me? I was supposed to start the dressmaking a week ago. How do I know they'll keep my place for me?

I've won, this time. I stick the combs in the high knot I've made, and kiss the back of her neck.

– There. See how pretty I've made you.

– I'm not your *doll*, she shouts at me.

I forget all about Rosina as soon as I leave the kitchen after our dinner and come out into the area, shutting the door softly behind me. Overhead the sky is blue and gold, early evening, the sun getting ready to vanish. I run up the steps, into the square. The light is cool and polished on the big sycamore trees, on the first fall of leaves, yellow and brown, on the dry earth. Hot colour of packed flowers glows in the half-moons of flowerbeds, a tight jostle of pinks and reds, low round blooms at my feet boxed by silvery shrubs. Like apples fallen in orchard grass. Shadowy grey-green of the trees, the little square of lawn, and these half-circles of colour sucking the last light of the sun into themselves, warming the garden while the sky goes cold, metallic, turns peacock-blue.

George is waiting for me on the iron bench under the plane tree. Behind him, lights spring up along the rows of houses, gold and amber oblongs, until the blinds are drawn. Minny's drawing room blazes bravely. She's inside there by gas and candlelight; I sit outside here in the chilly darkness, George's hands grabbing me to press my face into his jacket, my arms around him. No one can see us; we're deep in under the trees, private and safe, screened from the gas lamps that march along between the terrace and the railings of the square, part of the blackness. George turns my face up to his; his greedy mouth seeks mine. He opens my jacket and my blouse and puts his hands on me. Because I like it I let him, though I know I should not. The moon curves behind his ear. The tree rustles above us.

– We could get married, Florrie, he mutters into my neck: you want that? Let's get married.

I haven't told Rosina that George has turned his attention to me. Not yet. She misses him, and mopes, but she assumes she'll see him again as soon as we return to Hackney. If I told her now, she might fly off and leave me, and I can't stay here on my own. It wouldn't be proper.

– Not yet, I hiss at him: we'll have to wait. I can't possibly get married now. It would spoil everything.

My work in the evenings with William, for a certainty.

– Why? he grumbles: you keep saying that. Why would it? What would it spoil?

I pacify him with kisses, promises, then leave him to make his long way home. I slide through the kitchen, unnoticed by the servants busy sorting and washing a chaos of dirty plates and pots, and make my way up the back stairs to the first floor. A sound of women's voices from behind the closed drawing room door; the gentlemen must still be downstairs with their port and cigars. I climb the staircase to the second floor. The door of Minny's bedroom is ajar. As I glance at it, it starts to open further. Not wanting to be caught by her in my dishevelled state I whisk past, and up the smaller staircase to the attic floor. Just as I'm round the corner out of sight, I hear her voice, a dry whisper.

– So let me know. Everything. I'll be waiting for your letter. Remember, you've promised me.

Smothered laughter, silence, the rustle of a frock as Minny crosses the landing, the slither of her skirts dragging after her down the stairs. A pause. Her bedroom door closes softly. The smell of cigars and eau de Cologne, as her companion, after this small interval, prepares to follow her. I peer through the banisters, wondering why William should need to write his own wife a letter. The thought of William writing Minny love letters pleading to be let back into her bed gives me a jolt. But the person briskly crossing the landing and running downstairs to the drawing room isn't my employer. It's Mr Frederick Andrews.

Rosina's not yet asleep. She huddles in bed, knees up to her chin, her face swollen with tears.

– Don't think, she spits at me: that I don't know where you've been. Because I do. I'll get even with you. See if I don't.

*

For your recent letter, dearest Mamma, I thank you with all my heart. Such messages of affection, such words of calm good sense, will not easily be forgotten. But I did not quite like it that you felt constrained, in the interest of my little Flora's welfare, to suggest that by rescuing her from proximity to *fallen women* I was also, in removing her from her accustomed sphere, perhaps in danger of filling her young mind with hopes of social improvement doomed to be disappointed. I am too careful, I believe, and Flora too wise, I think, for that to happen. Indeed, we have spoken plainly upon the subject. She knows that her visit can only be of temporary duration and that, while eager to teach her all I can while she is here on domestic, social and religious subjects, I offer her only a temporary respite, only a partial retreat. Simply, it is my ardent hope to be able to find her a suitable position by placing her with one of the ladies of my acquaintance, as nursery governess perhaps, or something of that sort. For one so young, she is truly excellent with children. I never have to worry about the little ones while she is here to amuse them; Nurse grows quite jealous!

Flora herself, such is her modesty, is dubious about my plan; but I hope gradually to convince her that such a genteel occupation would be in the best interests of herself as well as of her family, by removing *her* once and for all from the noxious airs of Hackney, and by removing from her *mother* (who is not in the best of health), the onerous obligation to act as her chaperone at public seances. Flora could still very well, I have pointed out to her, hold the occasional *private* seance for her employer and such ladies of the latter's acquaintance as wished to attend; simply, by taking up residence in the household of some sympathetic well-wisher (such as I have been) she would be assured not only of a regular if modest salary but also of that respectful and polite treatment so necessary to one forced to make her own way in the harsh world.

My Flora is not, I hasten to add, impervious to my arguments. Only, I fancy, she has a strong mind of her own about the best manner of employing her divinely-sent gifts! On occasion I have had to check her impetuous replies, so indicative of the ardours of her young heart, and remind her gravely of the duty we all have to submit ourselves not only to the will of God but the wise experience of our elders and betters. At these moments she always listens to me with the sweetest docility and gentleness, so that I have no doubt of persuading her, in due course, to adopt my plan for her future welfare and to become convinced of its excellence.

For there is no denying that a medium's calling is an onerous one, and one which, if practised assiduously, is liable to render a young woman prey to great fatigue and the possibility of seriously weakened health. Having seen how exhausted Flora becomes after a seance (for her first two weeks of residence here, we sat together every day), how much, after she comes out of trance, she is in need of repose and care, just as though she were an invalid (which of course she is not, being normally blooming and robust), I have thought fit to limit the number of occasions on which she and I sit to invoke the spirits to just two or three a week, thus affording her ample time not only for rest but also for exercise in the open air and the performance of her usual employments that I mentioned before. I have been very careful, also, to expose her as little as possible to the curiosity and excited interest of those in my circle of acquaintance (and you would be surprised, I think, at how numerous they are) who take an interest in the great discoveries afforded by spiritualism and who, being informed of Flora's presence in my house and of her serious and well-earned reputation, would wish to attend our seances and gain the comforts and enlightenment that the practice offers its sober devotees.

There was an unfortunate occurrence during Flora's first week here, when Miss Andrews, rather unwisely I thought, brought her brother with her to call upon me. Flora being present, I was obliged to introduce her, and the young man's subsequent conduct, I am sorry to say, seemed to me to be governed more by admiration for the young medium's lovely person than by reverence for my description of the sacred messages she imparted. There was, additionally, a sort of familiarity in his attitude towards her which I could not at all like: Flora may derive from an unfortunate social milieu, but her calling, after all, has lifted her out of it and made her worthy of the respect one gives a lady. Upon my recollecting that I had mislaid my thimble and Flora quitting the room to search for it, I asked Mr Andrews whether he had met Flora before? Meaning this only as a gentle reproof, such as my friendship with him permits me to offer, I was not a little surprised when he answered that indeed he *had*, that as a journalist interested in all the topics of the day he had made it his business to attend one of her previous seances in Hackney. He was about to say more when Flora re-entered the room, upon which I deemed it best to change the subject. He went away soon afterwards with his sister, and I did not see them again until last week, when they came to dinner. Though they both most affectionately pressed me to visit them very soon, I was obliged to say that my condition no longer allows me to pay calls. My confinement being only a matter of weeks away, Dr Felton insists upon the cessation of all excitements.

For the first two weeks, however, as I have said, little Flora and I did explore together, almost every afternoon, some of the mysteries of that dim world beyond the grave. Since I was mainly confined to the sofa in my room (I write, now, from my bed, whither Dr Felton has banished me) we sat there, by the fire, the latter, as you know, being necessary to my health, so that I could not dispense with it, much as I should have wished to; there is no denying the fact that an atmosphere of near-total darkness is the one most suitable to the reception by the medium of the spirit emanations. In the event of our being constrained to sit by the glow of the fire, full spirit manifestations were impossible. I confess I was grievously disappointed not to be granted a second vision of my little Rosalie, though, as I pointed out to Flora, she was not to feel at fault in any way, for that vision is forever engraved upon my heart, and to wish importunately for its renewal would be ungrateful.

Flora thanked me for my forbearance; she begged me to believe that though the afternoon light seeping between the closed blinds and curtains might prevent the full 'bodily' manifestation of my beloved little daughter, yet, if we had faith and patience enough, we might be enabled to discover the consoling joy of hearing my little darling *speak*. Thus it proved. Oh! The awe and majesty of those hours in which I was blessed to hear of her love for me uttered by Flora's lips! The relief with which I heard of her eternal wellbeing in the arms of Jesus! The soothing balm of those tears produced by her assurances of happy repose in the fields of Elysium! The intensity with which her little voice, escaping through Flora's bloodless and parted lips, insisted that she *had not forgot*! The emotion produced by these disclosures was sometimes such that I was forced to terminate the seance and beg Flora to return to consciousness; at those times my overflowing maternal heart threatened to burst its bonds for joy. And so sensitive to the needs of her audience was my little protégée, so pliant and receptive her soul, even in those strange regions where it wandered, that she invariably came back from those far shores once I had slapped her wrists and approached my smelling-salts to her nose. At those times, believe me, our souls drew very close together; a wordless communication passed between us; we gazed at each other in a silent communion too full for utterance.

William, who sometimes sat with us of an afternoon when he could spare the time from his onerous researches at the laboratory, derived as much instruction as I from these Heaven-sent occasions. It was he who suggested to Flora that, having proved herself to our full satisfaction in the cabinet in her parents' house, she should release herself from the necessity of being bound; that proof of her willingness to comply with the demands of scientific experiment having been more than once afforded to his expert scrutiny, he judged it in her best interests to be allowed to fall into the trance state in the manner most adapted to her health and comfort. The use of ropes and sealed knots, he pointed out, was only advantageous to a medium upon the occasion of her wishing to assure an audience of sceptical or hostile critics of her capacity to produce full spirit materializations. Amongst friends such as ourselves it might now be dispensed with, particularly since our present field of investigation, during these afternoons, was that of clairaudience only. And though in the evenings, when Flora and Rosina worked with him in his study to produce those full materializations, one of which I was privileged to describe in a previous letter, one might suppose the bonds to be necessary, yet he was so far satisfied of the young medium's good faith and integrity as to place no physical impediments in the way of the full exercise of her mediumistic gifts.

With this reasoning I of course complied, and so did Flora after a period of the prettiest doubt and hesitancy. To us both she spoke most earnestly of her wish to continue these afternoon sessions that imparted such a benign influence to my soul still struggling with the aftermath of bereavement, but the combined influence of William and of my dear physician Dr Felton, enabled her to accept, after a period of reflection, that *I* must not be overtaxed by a too frequently repeated exposure to the strong bliss of hearing my little Rosalie's messages of love, and that *she* must not be tempted, by the affectionate promptings of her heart, so to devote herself to afternoon seances as to have no strength left for the important work she and Rosina performed in the evenings under William's exacting gaze. Our house, dear Mamma, is now become a laboratory! For my dear William, so selfless in his search for scientific truth, has prevailed upon Flora to take part in his research. Once she had *my* permission, she of course complied with his wishes. Her obedience is so sweet!

Of these evening sessions I will give you a full report, dearest Mamma, in my next letter.

Until then, all the love in the world from your daughter,

Minny.

My servants wake me early on the morning of my wedding day. My women wash me, anoint me, paint my eyes and fingernails. They wrap a pleated skirt of thin linen tightly around my waist, paint my nipples gold, then cover my shoulders with a veil of transparent linen, encrust me with gold bracelets, necklets, ear-rings, anklets, finger rings. Lastly, they settle the long black wig, curled and oiled, on my head.

Outside, the heat is already up. The air is a scented moist towel patting my skin, yet dry too, a breeze stirring it, aromatic. Holding my head high I pace along the colonnade under the golden canopy held up by my four nephews, towards the waiting barge, to the shrill joyous music of flutes.

My father awaits me in the temple's outermost courtyard. I kneel at his feet to ask his blessing. He raises me, and we go into the temple together.

Only the high priests and the dark stone gods witness the long ceremony in the small sanctuary aglare with torchlight. By the power of this mystic marriage I am utterly changed: I become Queen, I become my father's wife.

At night we hold a great feast in the palace. I sit at my father's side and drink wine from his cup. Together we watch the tumblers and jugglers, the naked dancing girls who bend backwards sinuous as snakes, palms to the ground, writhing, leaping heels over head, then arching forwards again to dance on their hands, black hair swinging loose. Three of them are amongst my father's favourite concubines. That one there, the golden-skinned one tying herself backwards in knots, her silky belly poking up while her feet chase her hands through her open legs and never cease stamping to the music, she is my chief rival. Tomorrow I shall have her poisoned. My husband is mine and mine alone. I do not compete with inferiors. I imagine her little hands clawing at her guts as the poison eats into her and green slime oozes from her swollen mouth, and I'm happy.

I know how to please my father as no concubine can: have I not dedicated all my life so far to discovering and enacting his wishes? Do I not desire him more than any other woman possibly can? Am I not his favourite, chosen and singled out to share his destiny? So I lean forward, touch his arm, meet his eyes for a moment and then lower mine.

In the privacy of our room I dance for him while he lies on the heaped cushions of the bed and drinks wine. I tease myself as much as him, delaying the exquisite moment when all my linen clothes are off and I'm lying under him, naked. He kisses my ears, mouth, shoulders, breasts, moves his fingers inside me, exploring, while I bite his neck, caress him to make him big. I'm impatient, don't want to wait, seize his arse with both hands and draw him into me, my legs flying up wide apart, my hips lifting, a rise and fall to meet his. We smile at one another, content not to be slow, to make the dance last as long as possible, though we have no control over the sweetness that rises up, swishes through us, breaks over our heads. My father holds me in his arms, and we rest awhile, before our next bout, graceful and vigorous, that leaves us gasping and laughing, but not sated; not until the dawn do we fall asleep, tangled in each other's arms.

*

I don't want to do anything. Except to sleep, and get through the days that way. I'm heavy and slow. I drag along the street to the Dining Rooms, where I cook with indifference. All my skill has deserted me: I bake stodgy flans, burn the aubergine fritters, curdle the mayonnaise, forget the lemon for pancakes. I drag home again, hating the customers, hating myself. The air hurts me: my skin has been torn off and I'm raw. I don't want you to touch me, I don't want to have to breathe, I don't want to have to speak in case I start crying and can't stop. I clench my teeth. I take the phone off the hook so that the old man who dials wrong numbers can't reach me with his insistence that I know him. The skin over my forehead and between my eyes is tight; clamped and stretched. It's an effort to take a bath, to find clean clothes. I hide my hair under a black turban, hide my body in your bulky black tracksuit, your black leather jacket. It comforts me to wear your clothes and smell you on them. To be back in black.

Why write it all down here? To make it real. To make the memory of this time real; should it pass.

For long stretches of my life, when I was younger, I didn't feel real. My method of arrival at my aunt's house didn't help, I suppose: as an abandoned child I wore a *cancelled* notice on my forehead. The nuns said my real Father was in Heaven, adored by angels; he awaited my arrival; that would be the beginning of true joy. But here I was, stuck on earth meanwhile, stuck with a body. Loathing mine for what was imprinted on it, I was grateful for the nuns' lessons in self-denial, mortification of the senses. But these didn't work: my body, alien guest, invaded my pure spirit, dragged my soul back down from where it floated, transcendent. At night in my white-curtained cell in the dormitory, my body clamoured for attention, possessed me. I wiggled my finger in my ear, and examined the sticky brown gobs of wax that emerged, I chewed my fingernails, I tugged springy dark hairs from my head, I winkled bogeys from my nose, I attended to the salt taste of tears, I crept to the lavatory to let knobs of shit fall away from me, to note my period imprinting itself redly on the soft sanitary towel. These were disgusting sins I could not specify in confession to the chaplain for fear of embarrassing him, for he, like the nuns, had got rid of his body; I lumped them together under the heading of impure thoughts, and was absolved. The sin that was too wicked to mention went unconfessed, unforgiven.

Although I reluctantly accepted I had a body, I didn't feel like a real person. I was a fake. Once I left school, I could see that people out in the world were real. They knew how to go about the business of living; they just got on with it, plunged into life and were carried along by it, lived by it. I stood always on the brink, wanting to jump into that swift current and swim yet not daring to, not knowing how. I stepped back and became the watcher, learning about life only from watching others. They did not pause, agonize, doubt; they rejoiced, fought, cried out with surprise or anger, suffered. I was lonely on the riverbank, seeing the swimmers shout and splash, but I did not know how to join them. Sex with all those men didn't help; I was always somewhere else when it happened, looking down at the two bodies on the bed. Sex with you feels real; both of us fully present to each other; but I don't trust it. Some strict patriarch in the sky is warning me off: don't *you* try to be happy, girl. You see what happens when you do?

It was through learning to cook that I finally broke into the world, joined it and was joined by it. At first food was just a drug to dull memory and pain. Then I discovered that flour and butter working between my fingers, carrots falling apart under my quick knife, egg whites rising in the bowl as I beat them, all began to give me a sense of my adequate power, my reality. Inventing then writing down recipes I unmade and remade the world, and, after a childhood in which I could not trust others' words, learned to discriminate, to speak. I discovered that it was important to know how to select and to classify, just as it was important to know how to combine, to unite, to merge. Through cooking I learned how to know when to separate and when to merge. Through cooking I learned how much I was part of the world around me, no different from leeks and peas, and how much I was separate from it, person not leek.

I imagined it must be the same with writing poetry: beginning with all the words in the world jumping inside in wonderful crystalline chaos, having to be sorted out, outside, into clumps and lines. I couldn't put all my favourite foods into one recipe, one dish: spinach aubergines mushrooms nutmeg artichokes cream olive oil basil parsley tarragon garlic rocket broccoli pasta lemons breadcrumbs capers anchovies olives onions rice sultanas cabbage; I had to choose. To leave some out. To experiment with complex and subtle combinations. This way I discovered what I liked and why, what I didn't like and why, and why this kept energetically changing. I was a baby discovering yes and no for the first time.

I felt like having a baby. I felt I *was* having a baby. That was so real.

You can't help me through this grief. You are there, peering over the edge of the pit, waving to me sadly, sending messages down in baskets, but you can't do anything for me. You are simply there. A witness. You don't accuse me of self-pity; you just wait for me to feel ready, in my own time, to clamber out again. Other people, I know, are impatient. A miscarriage is not a real death, is it? Not like giving birth to a real baby who then dies. It's Nature's way, they say briskly; it wasn't meant to become a baby, don't you see? Pull yourself together and get on with your life. They don't want to have to see someone suffering; it's a messy business. I embarrass even my close friends with my grief for someone I never met, someone who never got born. They suspect me of exaggeration, of faking, of hysteria. They prod my old fear about myself, that I'm not real. This pain is real all right.

This pain could feel real. But it's not only other people who would prefer me not to mention it. I myself don't want to have to feel it. It frightens me. If I give way to it, let go, unfreeze, start to weep, I'll never stop. I'll go out of control, a flood that will drown you and myself.

I just want to go on getting by, and, most of all, to sleep until it's over. Surgery under anaesthetic.

This morning I forced myself to the supermarket. The street bristled with rain, pushchairs, the corners of shopping-bags, knees. I shoved my way through the crowds, wanting to kick, curse, flail my elbows, shout. I wished I drove a chariot like Elijah's, with knives and flames on the wheels. Inside the steamy warmth of what seemed an indoor racetrack for steel waggons, the aisles were clogged with babies and children, riding perched on trolley handlebars, carried in slings, dragged along by the hand. So simple to buy one or steal one, stuff her into my carrier bag and make off home.

I stood in front of the rack of cleaning materials, unable to remember what I wanted. So far in my metal basket I carried a bunch of parsley, a box of candles, a tub of peanut butter. Heaven knew what we were going to have for supper.

An old woman wearing a shabby tight coat and a pair of brown furred bedroom slippers stopped next to me and tapped my sleeve. Her eyes were bright in her pinched face. She pointed at a can of polish.

– That's the one you want, love. Not this one. That's beeswax, see? Much better. That's what my daughter-in-law always says, you can't beat beeswax. Go on, love, you take that one.

She smiled at me encouragingly. I picked up the can of polish and dropped it into my basket.

– There, she said: that's right, love, you'll be all right now.

She pottered off. I started crying, there in the store, in between the dusters and the cartons of washing powder. Nobody minded; they stepped round me and let me be. Not that I let myself cry for more than a couple of minutes. I went back to the vegetable section, wiping my hand across my nose because I'd forgotten my handkerchief, and picked out the two freshest artichokes I could see, a tight frilly lettuce, some lemons, a few flat dark mushrooms with black ribs, a bag of spinach, some aubergines. Then I barged my way back through the children and the babies to the checkout.

The old woman was standing in front of me in the queue. I'm a snoop; I always peer at other people's wire baskets as we stand in line, to see what they've got, to imagine how they live. The old woman had bought catfood, streaky bacon, sliced bread, a carton of milk, a packet of digestives. There was more food for the cat than for her. I shifted my bulky largesse to my other arm. She caught my eye, looked down at my basket to check I'd still got the beeswax, smiled.

– Terrible nuisance having all that furniture to keep nice, isn't it? Still, when you've done it you feel better.

I stepped back into the street, began to walk home. The mad old woman who prowls this neighbourhood was sprawled in the doorway of the chemist's, head down on her chest, eyes hidden by her woolly hat, legs splayed open under her short skirt exposing the naked thighs above the gaily striped legwarmers, jacket unbuttoned revealing her long wrinkled breasts. The first time I saw her, soon after I moved in, I approached her with the timid desire to offer her money and to cover her up. Fear that her semi-nakedness would incite abuse or assault. Nobody loved, desired or revered her ageing body and she knew it, she snarled at me and spat and I backed off. Now I know better. I bought sandwiches and a carton of tea from the snack bar next door to the chemist, put them down beside her without speaking to her, without invading her furious space, and hurried away before she noticed me.

I came home. I've got a house. I've got a roof over my head. I don't have to sleep in the street.

I polished the little round table on high slender legs in the sitting room, the one you picked up cheap at a junk shop because it wobbles and is deeply scratched. I found a clean duster in the cupboard under the sink, yellow and fluffy; and I polished away until my arm ached. The table responded, acquiring a deep shine. Some of the scratches disappeared. When you came home, we ate the artichokes, sitting by the window at the little table, our knees touching, by candlelight. For the first time in a month I could taste what I ate.

The child's cry is a weak thread of fretfulness, almost experimental at first in its wavering, its halts and starts. Then, louder and more definite, the anguished emptying of lungs. I've grown up to the sound of children crying, but I've never got used to it. I can't bear the ache of it, the despair that no one will come and relieve the pain, the lordly rage of the infant tuning up to terror at being left alone for too long. The little ones at home used to cry like this sometimes. If Mother slept through it, worn out, I went in to pacify them, to pick them up, to see what was the matter. To stop them crying. For my own sake as much as theirs. Not just because I loved them and hated to see them suffer, but also because I couldn't bear to hear the evidence of their pain and so simply wished to stop it.

No one is attending to this child tonight. It wails unchecked, its panic increasing. A higher note. I sit up in bed next to the softly breathing lump that is Rosina, wishing she would wake too, for comfort. Nurse sleeps downstairs with the children; why doesn't she soothe her unhappy charge, feed it sips of sugar and water till it hiccoughs into peace, thrust a hard-edged rusk against its sore gums for the newly arriving teeth to gnaw, rub its poor stomach to bring up the wind? The nursery is on the floor below, but the wailing surrounds me as though the miserable baby were in the room with us, as though it hung from our attic ceiling, butcher's meat on a hook.

Morning will come soon. Already dawn is a dirty brightness at the window, the square far below is beginning its clatter, there's a stir and a thump from the maid's bedroom next door. The baby goes on crying. I hear its bubbling screech even as I lie down again and curve myself along my sister's warm flannelette back, stick my fingers into my ears. Then, quite suddenly, the crying stops, cut off in mid-flow, a gurgle or two, a choking, and then abrupt peace. I settle into my pillow, disquieted, open-eyed, sleep rendered impossible.

All morning I'm heavy with apprehension. The silver basket of fresh rolls on the breakfast table scowls at me; the stairs rise up at me to trip me when I haul myself back upstairs to splash more cold water on my face; the cotton curtains at the little window of our bedroom are too clean. There's nothing to hold onto. I wish for my hands to be firmly grasped and stilled, I wish for a blindfold on my staring eyes, I wish for a gag to separate my biting jaws. I wish for a raging toothache, so that I could creep back into my cold bed and just be ill. I'm used to this depression, I'm familiar with it at least, but I can never accept it. Tears stinging my eyes and I can't think why, cries erupting then strangling in my throat, an ache in the pit of my belly, a roar of hunger that can't be assuaged by food. I grow very big, the edges of me dissolve, I don't know where my skin stops and the cruel air begins. There's no solid Flora anymore, just a frown on a forehead, a foot wanting to kick, a huge head bobbing on a neck grown suddenly thin and long, a stretching and tearing of guts and muscles. Food would anchor me, but I can't eat. A glass or two of wine would tip me safely over into sleepiness, but the dining room sideboard is locked and my bedroom is forbidden to me in the daytime: I'm supposed to be with the children. Prayer would console me, but I no longer believe in prayer; not at these moments anyway. Prayer is asking for consolation and release, the way I was taught it; what's happening to me is a possession, a capture; too late for prayer to make a difference.

So I give in, as I've learned to do. I report to Minny as usual after luncheon with the newspapers, the post, my basket of mending. I stand in the doorway of her room, my ears clogged with disturbances, a shriek and whistle of air around my head, my stomach tearing itself in two. My spine sags with tiredness. Sharp weights dragging my eyelids down, the voices far away but hissing nearer now, the dark cloak of unconsciousness stalking close. I didn't ask to be a medium. It is not pleasant; I carry other people's suffering in my heart, I am a magnet for souls rushing irresistibly towards me and depositing in me their anguished histories. I translate the suffering of the living into joy; I let the dark tides of history drain out of me once more as the souls of the dead return to heaven leaving in my arms their sadness at separation; I carry the sorrow of the living and of the dead. No one who is not a medium knows what it costs to launch oneself as a bridge between heaven and earth; no one would do it if there were a choice; it is too exhausting. It thins my blood, it saps my life. At first I felt it to be a grace, and moved towards it happily, with gratitude. These days, it fills me with more and more weariness. Women like Minny suck at me, greedy for nourishment; they never wonder who will replenish me. Each time I go into trance I am changed, my stock of vitality diminished, my burden of knowledge and of sadness increased. The spirits increasingly give to me of themselves as I leave more and more of myself on the other side. A transfusion. I am increasingly a changeling. I am not the Flora I was a year ago. But who knows that, apart from myself?

I always feel like this before a seance, especially now, in this house, when I am working not only with Minny in the afternoons but also with William at night. The marrow is leaking out of my bones. I am a hollow stick the spirits blow messages down. I'm the speaking tube in this house in Bayswater, a corridor for others' voices. This is the spirits' way of making me ready for their work. I must be scoured, emptied out, hollowed by fire, burnt white as a bone. I am the cave they enter. I don't belong to myself anymore; I don't know who that is. I've given it up. I'm the earth they press into, the clay their potters' thumbs mark with deep dents, the fragile pot they fire then throw onto the floor. I break up into little pieces; they need me to; I can do nothing but wait, shattered. Will they put me back together again? I'll be a different shape, that's certain. A pattern I don't recognize, don't remember. They remake me, over and over. It hurts. It frightens me.

Minny of course knows nothing of this. For her I'm a higher version of a sentimental novel, a diversion to while away the long afternoons, an upper servant cautioned to bring her only bonbons and sweets. She stuffs me into her mouth, she swallows me down. More and more of me she wants, day after day. Her eyes are hooks; she reels me in; then she eats me. And it's true, I give myself up gladly to this work, I throw myself eagerly into the darkness and open myself to my spirit guests; I don't refuse them. I go on choosing to do their work, because they touched my forehead with fire at the beginning, because they made my own soul dance and feel at liberty. I don't know how to say no to them. Vacant possession I am; they move in on me. Yet today I'm sick of myself. I'm dreary. I know it's necessary, this depression. I go on repeating that to myself as I sit down in the armchair opposite Minny and try to relax enough to begin.

The little round table, cleared of its cloisonné boxes, separates us. We place our fingertips upon it.

There is grief in the room. A small dusty cloud of it breathing out of my mouth and nose, rising in the air between us to take shape.

The table trembles. The table wants to sob.

I can hear that child crying again. As her noise comes nearer, so I have to distance myself from the body suddenly slumped back in the chair, the rasping passage of breath, the locked eyes. I'm detached. I'm floating. I've made room for the little girl who will insist on visiting me, who comes back weeping night after night to wake and reproach me, to ask for justice. Her neediness plucks at me like rain on glass. Her sobbing asks for entry. I stretch myself, I snap, I break apart. She's got me now. Her voice, thin and reedy, her plaint coming out of me like spittle.

Mamma. Mamma.

Minny's leaning forwards, her face guarded, her hands a twist of anxiety in her blue silk lap. I have gone far away, yet I can see her clearly. I need to; her eyes and voice will bring me back down, when it's time, when her little dead daughter's gone again. Today I can't let myself go too far away; I am too scared I might not come back. I want Minny to hold me, to keep me safe. I'm lonely, too big, drifting high up, I need her to tug on my string, to reassure me she's there.

If I abandon myself with the utmost trust to this air outside time in which I'm tossed, I can sometimes hear what the spirits are forcing out between my gasping lips. Even today, when I've thrown myself open to them with such difficulty, when my darkness does not glitter but is thick with the pain of people still on earth, when they thrash me like angry winds, I can faintly hear the spirits talking through me. Today, again, it's that crying child. I cannot comfort her when she comes to me at night. She needs to seek out her true mother by day. Why does she come to me so often at night? I want her to let go of me. But she won't, she needs me too much.

Mamma. It's me.

A sigh, escaped from Minny or myself, I don't know.

Mother me. You mother me.

So cold, the draught at my back. Looking down from billowy air, I see the half-dead medium shudder with cold, hold out her arms rigid and stiff, moan. She is the point at which opposite charges, opposite impulses, spark and meet: life explodes into death, heat into cold, past into future. She jerks, a tree struck by lightning.

Mother. Smother. Mother, you smothered me. Mother, you smothered me.

In the medium's own body a death takes place. In the medium's body death squats and grins. It cannot be otherwise. All the world of the dead is held in her. I watch her mouth shake, as death speaks through her. Life has fled from her white lips, from her fixed limbs. I cannot feel sorry for her; it has to happen, and I am too far away to prevent it.

Now the child is in the room with us. She is solid; she inhabits the air. Squalling amongst the heaped blue silk cushions on Minny's bed.

That desperate woman, who held me down until I was still.

Then death is gentle in the medium, flowing out of her eyes and mouth, fizzing away from her fingertips. The medium's body is full only of relief now. She has given birth to the pain, she has set it free, she can collapse, loose, letting go the afterbirth of pain. Ready to return to herself.

Someone is shrieking somewhere in the room. Someone's cheek stings where it's been bitten. I must help Minny. I must rouse myself. She needs help.

She slaps me again. My eyes are open now. Her face is a red boil of horror. Her fingernails have scraped along the tabletop, leaving scratch marks. She slaps me again. I am her guilt. She wants to mash me to a pulp and get rid of her guilt that way. But I'm too strong for her. So is little Rosalie.

*

In my last letter, dearest Mamma, I promised, as you will recall, to furnish you with a full account of the important experimental work William nightly conducts downstairs in the library with Flora and her sister. I take up my pen, therefore, to fulfil my promise and to describe these sessions as best I may from the distance that has been imposed on me.

How much I regret that my weakness prevents my attendance! But William, with his customary regard for my health, has forbidden my removal from my room; I cannot think of disobeying him when I know that the restrictions he lays upon me are motivated solely by the keenest concern for the safe arrival of our new little one. It *is* hard, sometimes, to spend evening after evening in this manner, but, after all, I am used to it. I do not repine; it is the price I must pay for the privilege of marriage to such a brilliant and hardworking seeker after truth. And at least he is at home and not in that horrid laboratory. I always felt that the air there did him no good. I am proud, moreover, of how far he takes me into his confidence regarding the proceedings of these researches he conducts downstairs; *that* is no small compliment he pays me; it is to *me* he imparts the first fruits of his labours!

Very thrilling and awe-inspiring fruits they are too. The spiritual conditions in our household, of an evening, being so conducive to Flora's wellbeing and consequent receptivity (and I flatter myself that the climate of Christian mildness and benevolence obtaining here in Bayswater *does* perhaps surpass that known to the natives of Hackney!) I have not been at all astonished to learn that my little Flora has begun regularly producing full materializations of her spirit control (a control, dear Mamma, being the ghostly guide who takes possession of the medium during a seance and speaks through her) in a manner that William has been able to verify as utterly authentic.

What happens is this. Flora having disposed herself full-length on the sofa in the library, which room serves as 'cabinet', William retires to the study to await developments. You will recall that the library opens directly onto the study by means of a large pair of folding doors. Leaving these doors open, William can see

Flora's form, as she lies in her entranced sleep upon the sofa, at the same time as he sees her spirit guide rise up and walk about the room. He has been obliged to hang a curtain of thick blue gauze across the aperture between the two rooms, as the bright light he has specially erected for the purpose of the experiment, in the study, would otherwise shine too brightly upon Flora's closed eyelids and disturb the vibrations necessary to the spirit emanations, but the curtain is not so thick as completely to screen the unconscious medium from view. Miss Rosina, who acts as secretary to William upon these occasions, taking notes to his dictation of the teeming ideas crowding in upon his agile and fertile brain, is most happily able to be an additional witness to what I can only call a miracle.

Over these evenings of close and unremitting research, William has got to know Flora's spirit control quite well. The spirit world, he reports to me gaily, has similar notions of etiquette to ours: upon the first manifestation of the apparition, she advanced towards him in the most maidenly and modest way, with her eyes lowered upon the carpet, then bowed to him before turning aside to pace up and down between the desk and the window. William says that she is quite charming: she always appears robed in the freshest white, her little feet quite bare and her hair, only partially concealed by a white turban, escaping from it to hang unbound down her back. Her name is Hattie King, which name, she explains, she uses for the convenience of her unlearned medium, it being the closest approximation in modern English that she can find to her real name, which so far she has not deigned to tell us. She has indicated, however, that she comes from the remotest antiquity, and is of the most aristocratic descent, which, William says, he can full well believe, for her manner and bearing are distinguished by ladylike poise and dignity. Moreover, the nobility of her antecedents is demonstrated by the confidence and originality of her language and behaviour. Where Flora is modest and shy, Hattie is outspoken and articulate; where Flora is simple and ignorant, Hattie discourses brilliantly upon a wide variety of topics; where Flora rarely speaks of her deep Christian convictions, Hattie imparts mysterious hints of ancient gods and the mystical powers of certain arrangements of numbers in mathematics; where Flora has been nowhere and seen nothing, Hattie describes her travels across the Dark Continent; where Flora is invariably serious and even, sometimes, depressed, Hattie is sprightly and full of playfulness and jokes; where, finally, Flora speaks with the deplorable accent of her class and milieu, Hattie utters her speeches with an intonation as pure as my own.

I enquired further of William, of course, as to the full content of the spirit's utterances, being unashamedly curious to discover the whole measure of the wisdom she has to impart. It appears that she often discourses upon philosophical, mystical and religious topics, her interests ranging from the powerful secret influences emitted by the Great Pyramid (as a result of its design by men who were not only architects but also seers) to the esoteric teachings of commentators on near-Eastern mystical texts. Sometimes she tells stories of her childhood in a palace of glittering white marble; occasionally she recounts the exotic myths and legends of her unknown country of origin; rarely, she makes prophecies for the future. Most touchingly, from my point of view, she forgets not to transmit unfailingly cheerful messages from our many friends and relatives who have passed away to the Great Beyond. No more proof than this, to my mind, is possible: she is apparently acquainted with the most *trivial* but not the least *telling* details of our family life, in past as well as present generations. If her medium were an *evil* woman, I could not help exclaiming to William, what very terrible consequences might not ensue from Hattie's intimate knowledge of these sacred secrets of the human heart! Gravely he assented to this, yet pointed out to me his interesting discovery that, while *Hattie* is apparently so well-informed upon our family history, thanks to her dwelling in those mysterious regions beyond the grave, yet *Flora*, when she regains consciousness after her trance, has no memory whatsoever of what has passed in the intervening hour, and is amazed at the words and actions of her spirit control that William imparts to her. Rosina has kept a full and detailed record of the words of the majestic guide, as well as of William's conversations with her and comments upon her disclosures, and I mean to read it as soon as I can, once the devoted amanuensis has made a fair copy of her notes and transcribed her rapid scribbles, so like, to my eyes, the hieroglyphs of the ancients, into something more resembling a polished English style. For the moment my doctor cautions me against undue intellectual effort and stimulus, so I must defer the interesting perusal of Rosina's document to a later date.

These you see, Mamma, are the momentous events of our little household! They quite overshadow, I often think, the *other* interesting event we all await with such joyous apprehension. But of course I do not complain. I am attended with all the medical expertise I could wish, and I am sure it is no bad thing that William's devotion to his research, in which, as his wife, I share so fully, should take my mind off the hours of pain and peril which daily approach. My only regret is that William's attention to his work, to the near-exclusion of all else, should render him more fatigued than I like to see him.

In the mornings, when he comes in to salute me before departing to the laboratory, I cannot help observing how heavy-eyed he is. Once or twice I have even ventured to observe to him, in the most lovingly playful manner of course, that the spirits are no respecters of persons and should perhaps allow him a little holiday! But, as he never fails to point out to me with his calm good sense, it is Flora who is truly drained and exhausted by the demands of these regular seances, and *she* never complains, having such a regard for her patron and such a respect for the elevated nature of his scientific calling. To her I have merely commented upon the necessity of preserving her health, and she invariably agrees with me, and tells me that she never felt better in her life. She means so well! Yet I fear her temperament is rather a nervous one, rather given to flights of fancy and over-passionate response to kindly advice. I am afraid I distressed her the other day when I remarked that now that I am about to become a mother for the tenth time it was perhaps the moment to consider receiving no more messages from little Rosalie, in order to resign myself for ever to my loss and prepare my heart for the next little angel to occupy it. I had forgotten, of course, that Flora has no control whatsoever of the voices speaking through her from the grave! But it has become necessary for me to look *forward* now, and Dr Felton agrees with me. I softened my rebuke to Flora, on that occasion, by the presentation to her of a larger sum than usual. It is my custom after a seance, as I am sure I told you before, to show my appreciation to the medium by making her a little gift, for which she is always properly grateful. I ventured at first to give her some of my cast-off clothes of last season, but then, fearing to offend her pride, I substituted little presents of money saved from my housekeeping allowance.

If William knew that I were writing to you, he would of course send you all his love, to add to that plentifully supplied by the children; but he is hard at work in the study at this hour, drafting his essay on spirit materialization that he means to publish in the next issue of *The Spiritualist Magazine*. I forgot to tell you that he has also been taking photographs of the beautiful ghostly control, and very interesting and illuminating of his thesis he tells me they are too.

Pray for me, Mamma, as my hour of trial approaches! Pray for me that I shall pass through the dark valley of the shadow and return safely from it with a new, healthy little cherub in my arms this time!

Ever your loving daughter,
Minny.

Just before my father dies he opens his eyes and looks at me. I have allowed no one else to sit at his bedside and hold his inert hand. The physicians whisper in the corner and prescribe different drugs and treatments, the servants wash and tend him and force a little wine between his slack lips, but it is I who hold his hand and send my spirit coursing after his in the warm air where it wanders, almost free of its ties to earth. My hand on his keeps him with me, while I cry out to him in silence not to depart without some sign to me, some token that he knows me. For seven nights and seven days I sit by his bed, refusing to eat or sleep, not caring about my disordered hair, my soiled robes. Grief makes me impatient with my women when they approach me with a cup of milk, or wipe my hot brow with a cloth dipped in rose-water, or urge me to snatch a few hours' sleep. I am stronger than lesser mortals. Am I not the Queen? Must I not stand watch beside my dying husband? I slap the women's faces when they come too near or bother me too much, and bid them be gone. They break my fragile contact with the King.

In the middle of the seventh night my father opens his eyes and looks at me. Imploring. I bend over him, slip my hands under him, raise him so that his mouth is next to mine, his cracked, parted lips brush mine. His message is whispered, but it reaches me. It flies into my heart. He breathes out, a long expiring sigh, and his breath comes into my mouth. I take it in, I hold it inside me. He pours all of himself into me, then relaxes in my embrace. Though I lay him down, calling out and weeping, I am secretly triumphant. I have him now. He lives on in me.

After the splendid burial, after we have laid him in his home in the rock and sealed the door, I summon the high priests and chief officials of the kingdom to the palace. I receive them in the hall where I and my father sat together on our high thrones. Now there is only one throne, and I sit upon it.

My courtiers expect me to stand down as ruler of Egypt's two kingdoms in favour of that puny boy they have produced as heir, that arrogant prince who claims his right to become Pharoah by virtue of his royal descent on my mother's side. But I was not born of woman; I was born of the gods and of my father; my father dwells in me, not simply in the tomb; and I shall not yield.

So I sit in state and watch the most powerful men in the kingdom kneel at my feet. On my head I wear the high double crown of Upper and Lower Egypt. In my hands I carry the sacred sceptre and flail. On my chin I wear the curled beard-wig that denotes kingship. I am no longer Queen Hat, consort to my dead father. The man in me has come forth and must be recognized. I have done what no woman has dared to do before me: I have named myself Pharaoh of Egypt. Power over all this land while I am on earth, sole power; I, only I; and life everlasting amongst the gods when I die. I am man, I am Pharaoh, and I shall rule.

Yesterday I hated you all day long. I couldn't get down to work, I was so enraged and upset. I stormed about down in the basement instead. Snapping sticks for firewood, I broke your legs. Scrubbing the paintwork on the walls, I rasped your skin. Kicking the door shut, I bruised your ankles. Yelling at the cat, I insulted you with a fine stream of invective. You weren't there to be yelled at; you left early for an appointment with a gallery.

Hate is a house built on parched ground. Hate is a house fenced about with barbed wire and broken glass. Hate lodged in me, a sharp stone that cut.

Ever since the baby died I haven't wanted sex. Yet I remember it, how when you fuck me I feel so loved.

The nuns at the convent taught us that sex was acceptable only within marriage; sex was excused as the chaste and procreative love between two people sworn to eternal fidelity. Most of my male clients, when I worked as a prostitute, were frightened of emotion and came to me for what they called 'just sex'. The nuns believed that a woman controlled her man by controlling herself; the clients wanted to control me in order to control themselves.

It was the sex with you that made me begin to love you, not the other way round. Our two bodies talk, love, feed, play: sex. You never hold back; you pour yourself at me, you abandon yourself into me with trust, you give me all of yourself. I think about you; my cunt thickens and swells, I gulp and shiver inside. Love and desire slosh in me, liquid; I walk carefully, holding, not wanting to spill. You've melted me, you've made me runny and hot, I'm making up for cold years, years of starvation.

But I didn't hold the baby carefully enough. I let the baby slip out.

Yesterday I hated you because this house is falling down. This house is falling down because I hated you. The roof lets the rain in; the ground and first floors are still in the same state as when I moved in, choked with rubbish; the window frames are rotten; loose flexes trail from gaping holes in the plaster. Our attic rooms are more or less intact and warm because we've laboured to make them so, but the rest of the house is still a shambles. You tell me I must be patient, that we can't afford to have everything done at once, that we must go slowly with our restoration work, one step at a time. But you don't care as much as I do; you've got your studio organized, and you're oblivious of its ruined shell. You paint; canvases, not walls and doors. You can live happily with chaos; out of it you build your house on canvas. But I live outside the edges of your paintings; I see the dust, I feel the draughts. I want to create a pattern out of the disorder of this house, and I can't do it all on my own. You don't see the value of housework. Most of the time you don't *do* housework. Yesterday I hated you for that too.

Yesterday I hated you because you've forced me to pause, to accept the disorder and chaos of my life. Mine has been a history of breakages, of losses. I want to forget all that. I want a whole house *now*, perfect, shining, intact. You've gathered me up, all the bits of me, this rage too, and you've forced me to confront the fragments, cherish the gaps between them, the play of jagged pieces, reassemble them in new shapes.

When you're at work on a picture, you float through the studio, thinking so hard you're clearly not at all conscious of yourself, your whole body curved into a sort of smile. Intent, concentrated, gathered into a point, strongly in relation to the world around you, yet also detached from it, carrying yourself lightly, your big body light on your feet, your red hair standing on end, thinking about what you're seeing, what you're making. I love that quality in you: your capacity to *look*. Noticing the ghosts of advertisements on the sides of old buildings, the faded black lettering; noticing tiny details in the decoration of Victorian façades; noticing the way women have dressed to swagger in the street; picking out strange curves and shapes from all the material of the city. While you wait for the paint to dry, you sit at the far end of the studio, on your high stool, in your paint-spattered apron, like a burly housewife, relaxed, happy, contemplating the colours and lines you've made appear. Then you rise, prowl towards the canvas, brush poised like an arrow.

I hated you yesterday because you went away too soon. I was asleep when you got up early; no time to lie in each other's arms, no time for sex, no time to exchange words of love. I awoke to the sound of the telephone ringing and you shouting curses because you'd overslept and you couldn't find a clean shirt and you had to do the washing-up before you could use the sink for shaving. You stormed about swearing, as you discovered that what you thought was a clean shirt (washed and hung out to dry by me of course) was spotted with marks by the rain (you don't believe in fetching the washing in) and that your only other clean shirt had two buttons missing. You tripped over the cord of the iron, you lost your wallet, your heavy feet battered the wooden floor, you didn't care that you'd woken me up early, you threw your anger over me like dirty water, you shouted at me to get up and answer the telephone since it was bound to be for me. You didn't bring me a cup of tea or kiss me goodbye. You banged out of the house, leaving me with your anger. It hung in the room, stifling and poisonous.

It was all his fault. It was him, of course, on the telephone. He won't give up. I screamed at him to go to hell.

You came home in the evening cheerful: the gallery wanted to see some of your paintings. You hugged me, whirled me about, enquired about my day. I ranted at you. I told you I'd been hating you all day, and why.

I expected you to react according to the way you've been behaving towards me ever since the miscarriage: patient, tolerant, protective. But you dropped your cheerfulness like a coat and shouted back at me: that I freeze you out, that I'm completely self-sufficient, that I deny we're a couple, that I want to run everything, that I treat you like a tenant not an equal, that I'm obsessed with domesticity. A bloody feminine monster you said I was, an Amazon who doesn't need a man because she's got a vacuum cleaner to love, more like a sergeant major taking barracks drill than a lover, an ideal home mattered far more to me than a man, men were just bits of mess to be swept into corners.

I yelled back at you, but you weren't listening. In the midst of your anger you were crying. She was my baby too, you roared: why have you never admitted that, as though you made her all by yourself and I had nothing to do with it, why can't you allow that I also suffered when she died, that my grief is as real as yours?

So much fury in the room. We both shook with it, my fingers and toes tingled and fizzed, we punched and winded each other with words, until we were both crying, the room held us, separately, and shook too. Not until the middle of the night did we find each other again, making love in the darkness, in silence, warm, a violent giving and taking then collapsing into sleep.

This morning I awoke to someone singing about love and peace in a falsetto voice: you in your boxer shorts dancing a ridiculous opera, greeting your clean shirt, the iron, your shaving brush, with high squeaks of exaggerated pleasure, a burly nymph bounding on tiptoe, serenading me and the odd sock and the mug of tea. I lay in bed broken up by laughter. You smash through my defences; you know how to mend things too. You bounce back when I punch you; you don't sulk; you say sorry. You forced me to admit for the first time that I love you.

I've had many lovers. None of them stuck up for me fiercely, egged me on, enjoyed me, believed in me, listened to me, like you do. I'm used to men loving me then leaving: sorry dear I have to go to Argentina. You want to stay, and to make demands on me, and that frightens me. I'm not used to it. You are loving, and want to be loved, and you force me to confront the pain of loss. Past. Present. The possibility of future ones.

Yesterday in our bedroom I saw a little girl. She was blue. With terror not just cold. Her unspoken and unspeakable rage. Holding her breath in the dark as the bedroom door sneaked open. The shuffle of his slippers on the lino outside. A haunting I held at arm's length like a photograph that I wanted to destroy.

Yesterday when you wrenched yourself away from me in anger I felt as though my guts had been torn out. Our dead baby was torn out of my guts. My grief for her has gutted me and torn me up. My love for you contains all this: pain and grief and desire and laughing at myself and rage and lying close to you knowing you.

Yesterday afternoon, because I was too angry to work on recipes, I decided to make a start on the basement. I wanted to begin turning it back into a kitchen, to see whether the old range still works, to hear the true heart of the house beat once more. I scoured and scrubbed. I banged about between the walls with sponges and mops; I sluiced water along the stone flags of the floor in quick hard dashes; I knifed off fifty years of rich black grease from the sink and the stove and the wall behind. My impatience for transformation drove me until my knees sagged, my back ached, and I sat down at the table for a rest.

At first I thought it was a trick of the light, the mellow autumn sunshine streaming through the high dusty window panes and making patterns in the air. The room jolted, everything stopped: my breath, my blood. Then, with a click, inside me or outside me I couldn't tell, the room started up again, and I heard grains of dust fall onto the cold clean window ledge, the door of the stove settle into its hinges, the shelves of the dresser proceed in their ageing and rotting. I stood up, uncertain what air I balanced against, what dimension held me, how much I was solid and how much I was a loose collection of atoms mixed with the flow that I clearly saw made up what I was pleased to call a chair, a table leg. I was transparent and I dissolved; 'I' no longer existed; 'I' was just a linguistic convenience, not any kind of truth.

Something re-composed me and gave me eyes again.

There was a little girl there, sitting opposite me. She looked to be ten years old or so. Her fair hair fell onto the shoulders of her white linen pinafore in long curls, and her fingers were red with chilblains. Her brown stuff dress, made high and tight to the throat and wrists, was fastened with little black wooden buttons. Every so often she sniffed, and raised her hand to wipe it across her nose and eyes. Near her on the table stood a wide flat basket, made of what looked like woven reeds. The plaited rushes were still fat and fresh, as though recently picked from a bed next to a stream. They were still alive, they were still a juicy greeny-brown, they still had sap, they could still evoke water, an arc of sky with geese flying across it in a grey V. The child dipped her hand into the basket and brought out a fistful of bits of metal, twisted fragments. Pieces of broken type. She began to compose with them, laying out her words from right to left. She concentrated. I was sure she did not know I was there watching her. I thought her face needed a good wash; it was smudged with dirt and tearstains, as though she had recently fallen over perhaps, and only just stopped crying; she was still sniffing, sobs expressed as snot. I wondered who had picked her up and comforted her, who had told her to stop crying and be a good girl now, who had settled her at the table and provided this game for distraction. My own lap was empty, no child in it. I knew I must not try to touch the child sitting opposite me. It would frighten her. Time was a thin skin between us I could see through. Time enclosed her, a placenta. If I tried to puncture it, to reach through, I would do damage.

I used my eyes, not my hands, peering across the wood of the table top, whitened and smoothed by years of scrubbing, to see what word she was making with the letters she laid out so carefully.

HAT. HATE. HATE.

Silently her mouth worked, forming shapes of words. I read her mouth, I read the sounds she could not utter.

HATT. HATE. HATTE. HATTIE. HATE. I.

I must have protested, by some gesture, I must have startled the air. My disturbance reached her. Finding my face looking into hers, she dropped her bits of type, put a hand up to shield herself. Fear wrote itself on her face. Then she was gone.

No letter, message or telegram awaits me at the hotel desk. Shiny brown wood with a gilt rail, an aspidistra in a fluted green pot, a little handbell, all spell *abroad*, *abandoned*. I gaze at them to give myself time to think. Lifting my eyes to the mirror behind the desk I see, in its spotted blurry depth, the mask of a woman's face, set into tight calm, as though I've tied my face on like a veil.

Meeting the patron's gaze, curiosity pretending to be sympathy, I manage a shrug, a smile. Refusing to panic, far too soon for that, I concentrate on the immediate problem: why couldn't William have chosen a hotel where the staff speak some English? His insistence on discretion has meant I'm not allowed to travel with him on the train but have to go in the ladies-only carriage, I can't be seen talking to him on the boat, must stay in this pokey hotel in a backstreet where they speak only French and don't like foreigners.

Anger with William stiffens my back for me. I toss my head and pick up my umbrella from where I've dropped it on the tiled floor. *San fairy ann*. William gave me a phrase book; I practised on the boat, there being nothing else to do but talk to myself on the greasy deck under the stars, the wind salty and damp on my face, until seasickness drove me below to the rough care of the stewardess in the ladies' cabin. *San fairy ann, bong jure, silver plate, mercy*. If Rosina were here too we'd laugh at these strange sounds. But she's gone to stay with Aunt Dolly, furious and distraught now she knows George loves me, threatening to tell everything. I've paid her to hold her tongue about where I am, but I can't trust her to be on my side. Not any more.

France is as flat as Essex where Aunt Dolly lives. Rows of poplars, grey houses with slate roofs, cows at pasture, lines of willows along streams, thatched timbered barns. Seated in the train, I sing to myself to the music of the wheels: I've done it, come abroad all by myself with no one knowing.

I plod up the curving staircase after the maid's crisp black skirts, admiring her thin ankles, her curd of white starched petticoat above black stockings embroidered with black daisies, little high-heeled boots. My own stockings are ruined with seawater from the overflowing bilges on the boat; I promise myself I'll go shopping tomorrow and buy a new pair in real silk. *Bass*. I mouth the word to myself.

The maid vanishes, closing the narrow double doors after her with a click. She has dumped my bag on the floor, hasn't bothered to light the gas. I'm in a room that feels vast and empty as a church in the middle of the night. Then my eyes grow used to the dimness, and light piercing the crack between the shutters shows me the gleam of a polished wooden floor, two long windows draped with pale curtains, the edge of a fireplace. I slide along unfamiliar slipperiness, fumble my hand through layers of soft muslin to release the window catch, then pull the shutters open, wrestling with them until they crease back in folds.

Paris may be all around me but I can't see much of it: a narrow street lined with dirty grey façades, the wall opposite so close I can almost touch it, blank except for one ornate window masked by an iron grille. I saw nothing from the cab, either, its square of glass scratched and thick with dust. So I turn back inside, sniffing the queer smell of perfume and disinfectant, study the bronze can of dried pink hydrangeas in the marble fireplace, the yellow china clock and candlesticks ranged above it. Here's the bed, tucked behind the door; high and narrow, curve of blackened mahogany at head and foot, spread with a white coverlet. Here's the washstand behind a shabby brocade screen.

I unbuckle the straps of my bag, lift out my toilet things and my dressing-gown. Silver tops on my bottles of lavender water and witch hazel, real porcelain for my pots of tooth powder and rouge. I set them out carefully on the pink marble shelf, stroke them. Paid for all by myself, the best I could afford. With William's money, but I earned it. Just as good as anything in Minny Preston's dressing room, and I didn't have to coax or wheedle for them either. My slippers please me too, yellow satin ones bought new for this trip, gold rosettes of ribbon on the toes, black braid outlining the high instep. I have pretty feet, small and arched. Mr Redburn always praised them, George and William too. These slippers are flimsy things that won't stand up to much wear. But then I'll buy new ones.

Off with my tight dress. I fling it on the velvet stool. No stays: too much trouble when you've no one to unlace you. Long spars of whalebone sewn into my bodice do very well instead. I sniff my armpits. Sweaty. Too bad. I'll wash later. I piddle in the tin pot, then put on my dressing-gown, scarlet padding that fits snugly around my waist. I lock the door, then shuffle over to the bed, clamber up onto it. The coverlet is clean, but what a smell of camphor, as though it's lain in a cupboard all summer through then not been properly aired. I let my head fall back on the big square pillow, having thrown the long sausage-shaped bolster onto the floor. I'm so weary. I touch the crisp lace frill, promising myself a rest of half an hour, then I'll go down, brave the dining room, get myself some supper. I fall forwards instantly, into a pit of sleep.

The clang of church bells wakes me. My eyes are wet with

tears. I heave up onto one elbow, chilly and uncomfortable, staring at the bright sunlight pouring through the window. It's morning. I've slept for twelve hours. I remember my dream. Finally, I was going to find out. But the bells have beaten me out of sleep with their golden tongues, and I'm in a strange hotel in Paris all by myself with no idea of what to do now and I'm starving hungry.

I ring for the maid and manage to make her understand what I need. A tin bath arrives, followed by cans of hot water, a tray of coffee and rolls. A fire is lit. After my bath I wrap myself in an enormous linen towel, sit down in the armchair with my feet up on the little stool, the velvet soft as a cat's belly on my bare feet. I rub my feet back and forth over fur, voluptuous. Surely William will arrive soon. We'll drive in the Bois de Boulogne, we'll eat delicate cakes filled with almond paste and chocolate cream, we'll go to the music hall and dance together, we'll stroll by the river in the sunlight arm in arm. I repeat this to myself several times, to stop other thoughts from nagging at me.

Then there's a knock on the door, and William's in the room. I don't jump up. By now I've learned a lot about what he likes. I stare at him, licking coffee froth off my lips with the tip of my tongue. He locks the door behind him and leans against it, watching me.

With him in Bayswater, certain gestures, certain movements, were never permitted. His was a house in which I never felt relaxed; I was always worried about making a noise, laughing or speaking too freely, taking up too much space, soiling the carpets with my boots, crushing the cushions of the chairs when I sat on them. I had to be stiff. In public, I mean. When Minny was there. My body could not fit in that house. At night it was different, when it was just him and me together, Rosina having gone to her room and all the others asleep. Then he liked Hattie to move freely, to dance even, if she felt like it; he thought that was what I was like amongst my own people in Hackney, he expected a certain coarseness. It excited him. Also it allowed him to stay cold, in control.

He's a cruel man when he wants to be, I think now, watching his long fingers clench and then jam into his pockets, his long back tilted against the closed door, his long legs nonchalantly crossed, his eyes weighing up my semi-nakedness. There's no reason, I tell myself, to be afraid.

– Get dressed. We're going out.

I stand shivering in the middle of the floor, pulling my chemise over my head. I haul on a stocking and tie my garter.

– Hurry up.

He smiles at me. A false smile, made with an effort.

– Let's not waste this fine morning, my dear. I promised to show you Paris, and I shall. We're going to take a walk together, and then I'm going to show you one of my very favourite places.

Your notes and letters, my dearest Mamma, over the last few weeks, have been for me an unfailing source of comfort. You are not surprised, I know, that I have been unable before this morning to take up my pen to write to you; you recollect, I am sure, the weakness that always assails me after these happy events; and I know that William has written to tell you of our new little daughter's safe arrival in this world, and of our corresponding joy. My sufferings, as usual, were frightful; words cannot express what I endured; it is better perhaps, to draw a veil over them. At this moment, I will admit to you, I would not willingly pass through that agony again for the world, particularly since it has left me afflicted with a lethargy and depression I have so far found impossible to throw off. William, as well as Dr Felton and Nurse, attended me; all witnessed my anguish during those frightful hours; but no one, of course, could comprehend the extent to which those terrible pains racked me. William, indeed, was a most faithful attendant, holding my hands in his, cheering and encouraging me, bathing my brow with water. Dr Felton has prescribed rest and tonics; Nurse has taken the care of my little newborn infant completely off my hands (she has found an excellent wetnurse); so that, after a period of adequate repose, I may expect to be back to normal. At the moment I have not the energy for anything. It is only to be expected, I daresay! To *you* I may whisper what I dare confess to none other for fear of being thought over-excitable and nervous: that the melancholy I suffered from *before* my confinement has, I am sure, in no little measure contributed to my prostration *after* it.

To continue in this vein doubtless displays the weakness and self-indulgence consequent upon my present state of invalidism, yet I cannot prevent myself, dearest Mamma, from pouring out to your tender and solicitous ears some of the miseries that at present afflict me, in the hope that such a release of my over-charged heart may assist me in the recovery of my health and spirits. I cannot confide in Dr Felton as I should wish, patient as he has always been with my infirmities, for he begins to look grave and to talk of neglect of my responsibilities when I insist, as he puts it, on remaining in my bed after the normal period, and naturally I do not wish to burden William with extra worries when he is so busy. Nurse has an excellent and most amiable heart, but in a person of that class I cannot of course with any degree of openness confide. And Miss Milk being so young, I could not dream of making *her* my confidante. In any case, she has departed, along with her sister, on a visit to her aunt somewhere in the country, near Essex I believe, and we are not sure of the date of her return. Her going was agreed by us all to be best, for reasons of delicacy, my feeling that a sickroom so soon to be the site of childbirth was not the best place for a young girl of Flora's impressionability. She protested, with many affectionate smiles, that the conditions of her unfortunate upbringing had made her not unfamiliar with the mysteries of maternity (the house of her parents being so small as to have rendered it impossible for Mrs Milk's older children not to have heard, and comprehended the reasons for, their mother's groans) but, as I observed to William on that occasion, though I might miss her bright company and her assistance with the children, yet I could not fail in my duty, as her patroness and chaperone, to shield her as much as I could from events of which, at her age, she should properly be ignorant. William heartily concurred with me, I am glad to say, especially since his researches into Miss Milk's mediumistic capacities are now finished, enabling him to prepare for the next stage of collating his results with those of other practitioners in the field.

I am, therefore, more alone and friendless than I have been for some time, since I am not yet well enough to receive visitors or to venture out to visit my acquaintances. Mr and Miss Andrews have called several times, but I have not felt like seeing them. To you only can I recount the disturbance of my present condition; in you only can I trust; from you only, I believe, shall I receive sympathy rather than reproaches!

Know then, dearest Mamma, that I have been suffering not

only from physical disability and from a depression, which, as I said above, I am *unable* to recover from, but also from the most terrifying nightmares. These commenced about a month before I was due to be confined, and have not ceased with the blessedly safe delivery of my little one (who, I recollect that I have forgot to tell you, is the sweetest and bonniest of babes). I assure you that I do all in my power not to dream: I compose my mind with the utmost religious solemnity before lying down, I fail not to pray morning and night for the grace to be delivered from this trial, I take all the medicines that Dr Felton prescribes with his kindly optimism, I eat all the meals that he recommends me and drink all the warm milk he advises me to swallow. Yet the dream recurs. It is always the same one. The prospect of its arrival so torments me each night that I grow increasingly unwilling to close my eyes! Yet such is the power of my sleeping-draught that I invariably fall asleep quite quickly, the drug's action working also to ensure that I cannot awaken before I have passed through what seems like weeks of horror.

In the dream I am standing, with William and all the children, in the nave of an ancient church, attending a religious ceremony that seems to be a funeral: we are all clothed in black, and the expression on my companions' faces is uniformly one of sorrow. From here the scene shifts to a desolate and barren landscape: burning red sand underfoot, a pitiless foreign sun in a sky of bronze, the bones of dead animals scattered about, and, here and there, the gigantic ruins of what might be temples or palaces, half silted up with sand. I am alone here; the children and William are lost to me, I know it, for ever; I wait, in dread, for the approach of some monstrous being that lurks behind one of the toppled colonnades; I smell his rank smell, I hear the scrape of his claws and the grinding of his foul jaws.

When the figure of Miss Milk, dressed all in white, approaches me from one of the crumbling stone doorways, I stumble towards her with relief, my arms outstretched. She is more charming than ever, her long curls blowing in the wind, her light muslin robes gathered about her with effortless grace, a white veil, like a bride's, thrown back from her smiling countenance. Then I perceive that in one hand she carries a bloodstained kitchen knife, and in the other, the torso of a human child! As I halt in terror, she raises the ghastly piece of flesh to her mouth and begins to gnaw at it, looking calmly at me all the while. And

Then I see that the victim of this hideous cannibalism is none other than my very own newborn babe!

And as I start back, so she changes, becomes half woman, half beast. Her hair dissolves to the tangled mane of a lion, her feet and hands arch into claws. She settles herself on the sand like a giant cat, my dead child between her paws. She is the Sphinx. She stares at me with her terrible animal mask, and she waits.

I implore you not to think your daughter wicked for being subjected to such ghoulish visitations. I implore you to pray for me, and, indeed, to think of visiting me soon. Christmas draws near; will you not think of making one of our family party? Your presence will dispel my gloominess; your cheerful countenance will put these morbid phantasies of mine to flight; your strength of mind will help me compose myself to the contemplation of my normal affections and duties. In the anticipation of this balm I grow calm again. I have been too long confined to this sick-room; that is all that is wrong with me, I feel sure.

William of course sends you all loving greetings. He is busy packing up his papers at present, in readiness for the journey he must make tomorrow to Paris, whither he is bidden by no less than the great Dr Charcot, whose work at the Salpetrière Hospital with patients suffering from nervous diseases has long commanded William's respect and admiration. It is unfortunate that the summons comes just now, given my fragile state of health and William's concern for my loneliness during his absence, but I have accepted, as I must, that the claims of a wife and children (for he could not dream of my tearing myself away from my newborn in order to accompany him) must come second to those of science. William is not taking a holiday of course: he will be shut up inside locked wards; he will be contemplating those poor unfortunates smitten by all sorts of enfeebling and often incurable disorders; yet I am sure the change of air will do him good. Having completed his report for *The Spiritualist Magazine*, wholeheartedly endorsing Miss Milk's mediumistic capacities as genuine though still inexplicable by science, his plan is now to compare the physiology of persons endowed with mediumistic gifts with that of those afflicted with hysterical illnesses, having some intuition that the two conditions may, at certain points, overlap, and thus enable him to pursue further, as his next project, certain of his conclusions about a medium's unconscious mind. This is all very fascinating of course, and, equally, William cannot possibly relinquish the opportunity to discuss these matters with such a great man in his field as Dr Charcot, nor the privilege of observing at first hand the strange antics of his patients. When he returns, we shall be able to prepare for a real family Christmas, one at which I hope you will also be present. In the happier frame of mind which the prospect of that event induces, I take my leave of you, dearest Mamma.

Ever your loving daughter,
 Minny.

By day I am busy with affairs of state. Surrounded by the wisest and ablest men of the kingdom who revere me as a god, I consolidate my power. Also I cause to be raised many new buildings in Thebes, and, at Karnak, the highest obelisk ever to be seen in Egypt, all of them monuments that will attest to the greatness of my reign. The most splendid of these is my mortuary temple that rears itself proudly under the lofty cliffs across the river, the most noble structure ever built in the history of my people. A central ramp mounts through portico after white portico to the highest level, and in the middle court, behind the colonnade of white limestone, I have my architects design sculptured reliefs depicting the major achievements of my reign. At the beginning, my miraculous conception and birth; towards the end, scenes of my famous and exemplary voyages abroad. There is the bearded chieftain of Pwene, with his hideously deformed wife, abasing himself before my messengers bearing my emblem, saluting me as King of Egypt, female Sun who shines like the solar disc. There are my envoys presenting gifts of beer, wine, fruit and meat, and receiving in turn the valuables due to our great status: myrrh trees, ebony, gold, baboons, and leopard skins. I reward those counsellors who carry out my wishes: I grant them permission to be buried at the edge of my great court, I grant them sarcophagi of quartzite and priests to serve their sepulchres. Likewise I punish those who disobey me or who flaunt my patronage too openly and seek to exploit my favour: I mutilate the reliefs carved in their tombs, I erase all mention of them from the cartouches there, I forbid their spirits ever to find a dwelling place near mine.

By night I build more palaces, go on more journeys, push back the boundaries of my empire ever further. I soar in the darkness, I rejoin my father as he travels in his boat across the heavens along a track of stars, I follow him when he tips over the edge of the horizon and enters that uneasy underworld where his great sun is swallowed up. Night after night I trace the circle of his journey, to ensure that I wake in the morning, and that my power is secure. And day after day I erect myself in granite, in limestone. Incorruptible, undecayed.

Yesterday morning struck cold, the first day of winter overlapping with the last one of autumn. We dodged from the warm quilt and each other's arms in bed to the coal fire we built hastily in the sitting room. A fire in the morning; delicious luxury; signalling Sunday. Through the window the world was unexpectedly big and empty and bright. The glass sparkled with, suddenly, little beyond it: the leaves almost all gone from the trees, those left hanging withered and rusty, transparent in hard sunlight, a steely blue sky. Happiness was simple, animal; the room enclosing us, the window connecting us to the outside and to the sky, the warmth of the fire, a large French cup of painted porcelain steaming with fresh black coffee, the rough ribbed wool of your sleeve when I rubbed my face against it, my bare feet on the carpet, hot sun on my toes, the smell of sex I hadn't washed off yet because I so like it, a sixteenth-century Gloria pouring forth in exultation from the record player.

You're not a stranger. That's what I thought, looking at you, big red-haired man in your bulky dark sweater and tracksuit trousers, bare feet in Chinese slippers, no shirtcollar hiding the beautiful nape of your neck, bare and round, inviting my kisses. We're of the same species. We're kin. We're different in many surface ways, but deep down we are alike, we're made of the same substance. We change each other; we make an exchange; I've become part of you and you of me; yet we are still two people.

This morning I trusted sex again, more deeply than before, I trusted you and myself and what we make between us, the four-legged four-armed grunting gasping body, lusty hot cheerful, with your cock inside me I get confused forget which of us is which just darkness that has red in it and is ribbed squirming a pressure wetness new gestures we invent then forget crying out. Then collapsed on the pillows, your mouth on my neck, arms round each other, you're a big lazy cat stretched out long, you smack me through the duvet with your velvet paw and I smack you back, you shout for scrambled eggs on toast and mugs of tea, you shut your eyes, grinning, you put on a meek pathetic voice you're starving and you can't cook, you know I'll give you what you ask for, I smack you again then get up to make breakfast, we eat in bed sharing the papers you've dashed out to buy while I beat the eggs. Though we're separate again I'm linked to you by an invisible rope, warm umbilical cord of sex, first you fill me with pleasure then food does. So I sat and looked at you and thought: we are alike, we know each other's insides, we are at home inside each other.

After a late lunch we went for a walk around the cemetery, hip to thigh, your arm around my shoulders, my arm around your waist, both of us liking a rhythm of long steps, strolling in time with one another. Making love made the world look different: I realized that I was seeing double. With one eye I saw everything connected to everything else, a jumping mass of life I could not observe because I was part of it, merged with it; and with the other I saw a hundred different colours, precise, sharply separate. I saw the path dividing the grass, and the grass pressing in from either side upon the path, I saw the black branches of the trees cupped around the wind, full of it, and I saw the wind pressing into the black weave of the branches, filling their hollows.

It was truly the start of winter.

The cemetery was long swathes of iced greeny-grey grass, the path round the lake deep in sodden leaves under thick clusters of willows, an ornamental cherry tree burst open like an umbrella throwing off red darts, red rain, drops of red fire. An overgrown garden, narrow sandy paths threading between closely massed headstones and crosses and statues, between bushes ablaze with scarlet hips and haws, between tall bent trees whose leaves drifted down, soft and yellow. The air smelt of damp earth, rotting leaves, woodsmoke, rich and fresh. A garden big enough to get lost in, creeping down long alleys of stone angels, where the trees met overhead, where the brambles closed around sunken mausoleums and sucked them deeper down, where the long cold grass, beaded with moisture, waved across blurred inscriptions in stone.

Not a melancholy place; a sensual one; stars of colour among the dull greenery; all the wet green rot was so very alive; and the sun was fat and golden, its sweetness running down us.

We pushed into the older part of the cemetery, the Victorian necropolis. Ancient Egyptian city half buried in creepers and nettles, walled by oaks, broken columns, the backsides of tombs built like little palaces. Narrow streets led off at right angles from each other, lined with houses for spirits that tilted, propped each other up. Doorways and windows faced with blank stone. High oblong vaults like those the pharaohs and their servants rested in, tapered doorways to that other, invisible world, guarded by stone jackals and lions and sphinxes, braced by tall obelisks. Ivy wove it all together and stopped it toppling; we halted in the shadows under the cold gloom of a yew tree, the squelch of gravel and mud. No flowers here, no wreaths; just dark moss and the overhanging dark fringes of trees and the silence like cement between slabs of dark stone.

No one else was about. I sat down on a fallen tree to shake a pebble out of my shoe. Straightening up from re-buckling the strap I listened to the wind, caught the cold eye of a crouching beast, half griffin and half woman, and shivered. I put my arm around your waist and walked us out of there. I wanted to see a cheerful vulgar modern grave. I wanted green marble chips and pots of pink china roses. Not these bulging columns in the shape of palm trunks, of bound reeds, their plump capitals carved as lotus flowers, as closed lilies. Not this stone swamp haunted by stone alligators with cruel snouts.

The path ran along a crumbling wall draped with ivy dark as widow's weeds. A large tombstone stopped me, because the lettering on it was so beautiful; Roman, still sharp, well-spaced and well-cut. I stooped, pulled away a long arm of bramble to read the full inscription.

TERENCE MILK. 1830–1870.

Below it another name.

HESTER MILK. 1835–1877.

Round about, half-obscured in the busy undergrowth, were several little white crosses, marking the graves of children who had died young, three of them. Mixed in with these was a handsome slab of black granite with gold lettering. We bent down to peer at it.

ROSINA REDBURN. 1856–1922

BELOVED WIFE OF CHARLES REDBURN, d. 1881.

Next to it, in a plot busy with couch grass, was a plain cross in yellow wood, its lettering already blurred.

FLORA COTTER. 1854–1934.

WIFE OF GEORGE COTTER. 1850–1889.

We sat down on the edge of a stone urn and looked at the graves. They were personnel filing cards stuck in the earth. An attempt to classify and to keep separate bodies which were now dissolved into each other and into the soil holding them. The stone angels behind them bounded upwards, athletic, bored. Their index fingers pointed resolutely at the empty sky.

– Flora, I said: a good old-fashioned name.

I watched you test it, roll it over your tongue.

– Flora, you said: I like it. If we have a daughter the next time you get pregnant let's call her Flora.

You put your arms round me. I touched my lips to your cold neck. I saw late roses blooming scarlet in the withered khaki hedge, yellow leaves on brown mud.

Cotter, I wondered. It's not that usual a name. Could she have been related to my Miss Cotter?

– Though I'm not sure how, I said aloud: Miss Cotter was over eighty when she died, but even so. This can't be her mother. Her grandmother, perhaps?

I was pleased we had found the grave, I didn't really know why. Partly from the feeling that makes me prefer the idea of burial to that of cremation. I'd rather rot among the worms than burn to ash in an incinerator. I was glad Miss Cotter's relative, if she were a relative, had been put in the earth, that that trace of her was left, her name carved on wood that would erase itself in its own good time.

Your hug became a grip, demanding.

– Hattie. What about these phone calls? What are you going to do about them? That poor man. He's been really patient. I know you don't like answering the phone, but still. Those boxes in the attic *are* his. You'd only have to let him in for ten minutes.

We'd had this conversation several times. You knew why I didn't like answering the telephone. But I needed you to push me. I looked at the graves, ashamed of my cowardice, and came to a decision.

A gust of wind chilled my face and hands. I stood up, pulled you to your feet, and we returned home.

The telephone was ringing as we came in the front door.

You looked at me. I unbuttoned my coat and threw it over the banister.

– I'll answer it, I said: you go and see to the fire. I'll bring up some coal in a minute, go on, I'll get it.

After I'd put the receiver down I made for the basement to fetch up the coal. That was my excuse. I knew a third ghost waited for me down there. I'd heard her calling for me as soon as we came in from the street, a wail of anguish that pierced me, and I hurried to her.

The kitchen was lit by a single gas jet on the wall by the door. It burnt low, leaving shadows thick in the corners. The fire in the range was out; damp and cold had reclaimed the air. The remains of a meal, crusts of bread and a heel of cheese, had been pushed to one end of the table. A spoon stuck out of what looked like a basin of cold porridge.

My eyes searched for the child I could hear but not see. I hovered, uncertain, unable to make out the source of the crying, the kind of sobs that begin as simple grief and then become fuelled by terror. Howls of animal desolation.

Then my feet discovered where to go: they took me across the room to the big oak cupboard built into the angle of the wall next to the dresser. I turned the key in the lock, pulled the door open, and saw her, a little dark heap on the floor. I stooped and grabbed her, brought her out of there. I sank down on a wooden chair by the table and held her close to me, my arms wrapped round her as she stormed and shook. I couldn't think of her as a ghost. She was a real child, solid on my lap, her head pressed against my breast, her arms clutching me, her mouth against my sweater. There was snot crusted beneath her nose, and she smelled of urine. Her tears ran onto my hands, hot and wet. I felt her pain as keenly as though it were my own, I wanted to comfort her and take her pain away, draw it out like a splinter, kiss the hurt place to make it better. But all I could do was hold her to me, hope she felt safer crying on my lap than alone in the dark.

I kept her in my arms and listened to her sobbing. My body was made of love and it was all hers if she wanted it. I poured out words of love to her, I told her she was safe now, she was all right, I was here with her and she wouldn't be left alone. I babbled. I don't remember what I said. Her pain was the most real thing I'd ever felt and I held it as I held her.

As her gasping tears slackened, so she relaxed against me, tired out. She put her thumb in her mouth and sucked on it. In her other hand she clutched a sodden blue rag. She didn't seem to care that she didn't know me, I was her armchair and she rested on me. The storm past, I could study her white linen smock and flannel leggings and wonder why yet again I was dreaming about a ghost in Victorian clothes. Her fair curly hair was damp with sweat. Her eyes closed. She breathed gently against me. She was a thin child, four years old perhaps. I wanted her to be mine. I wanted to take her upstairs, into the warmth and the firelight. I wanted to promise her she'd never be shut up alone in the dark again. I knew I was dreaming, and that I'd have to let go of her as sleep let go of me and pushed me towards wakefulness.

I wasn't asleep and daydreaming. I heard your feet on the basement stairs, your voice calling me. The door opened and you clicked down the switch. Light leapt up all around me and dazzled me. I blinked. My lap was empty and the child was gone. All that remained of my visitation was the damp blue tea-cloth I was twisting between my fingers.

You decided I needed some looking after. You went out to buy a bottle of wine and a takeaway supper, you settled me in the big armchair beside the fire with instructions not to move till you got back, you embraced me then clomped whistling down the stairs. I shouted after you not to hurry, to stop off at the pub for your usual early evening pint, I'd be fine, I needed time to think about what had happened.

I stared at the fire, the coals you had coaxed and breathed on, built to a basket of clear molten red. Inside me was my childhood, alive and demanding, the little girl I'd been frightened of giving space to because of what she made me remember. Now it was time to remember, to admit her truth, to recognize and cohabit with it.

I dozed. You woke me, returning home with a big bag of pistachios, takeaway pizzas, a pineapple, two bottles of red wine. You draped the little round table with a white cloth, arranged on it a vase of flowers, two red candles in china candlesticks, two sturdy wineglasses in green glass. You turned out the light, lit the candles, poured out the wine. We sat opposite each other, lifted our glasses, drank. I splashed a few drops of wine on the cloth, sprinkled the stain with salt, watched the soft pyramid turn pink. We cracked open the green nuts and bit into them, throwing the shells on the fire, which crackled and flared. Then we ate the pizzas. We left the pineapple, spiky and yellow, and lay on the floor in front of the fire. By the light of candles and the grate's apron full of red coals you stroked my waist and hips and slid into me, your hands holding and lifting my arse, you filled me up as much as I wanted, on and on, no room left for ghosts or for alien hands. Then I lay against you, my head on your chest and your arms around me, I rose and fell to the rhythm of your breathing, held in your warmth. I didn't have to move, I didn't have to go away, I didn't have to get up and do anything, I could lie in your embrace, utterly relaxed, for as long as I wished.

At the turn of the stairs I pause. An oblong of bright blue lies on the uncarpeted floor of the little top landing. An oblong of blue light floats on the wooden boards. I can dip my bare foot into it and see my toes washed blue. More blue is thrown across the wooden banister, a long strip hanging like a gauze scarf, cool on my hand. My hand dissolves when I put it there. Blue washes me out, replaces me. The window on the half landing, at the turn of the stairs, has a small pane of vivid dark blue glass at each corner. The sun of early afternoon throws blue in bright transparent oblongs on the floor. Blue slides up the stairs after my ankles, and holds onto me. Blue water. All through my childhood this is a favourite game: to let parts of me enter the blue light and then withdraw from it, to let my hands and arms go blue, to dip my face in blue, to let cool blue light caress my head and neck and then pass over me. Blue comes and goes; I can come and go with it; I can make it come and go. It is always there for me when I return to it; it waits for me. Blue is my comforter.

The name of the hospital is enamelled in blue. Large letters with a dark blue shine. La Salpetrière. I will go on. I will force myself to write down what happened. I will go back in there, and remember.

I know I must confront my mother. So I walk down the stairs in my bare feet, out of the oblong pool of blue, I spiral down-wards, and I arrive in the kitchen where she sits hunched next to the stove.

From one corner of the kitchen table dangles a blue-checked

kitchen cotton cloth, the one that Mother uses for drying the glasses and the knives and forks. Flung down carelessly, it has just missed falling onto the floor, caught by an angle of wood. Flaring blue. A blue flag. A blue warning.

Her hands tumble loose at her lap. She is not working. She is just sitting there. She looks at her hands as though they're two dead rabbits to be skinned and chopped.

– You're supposed to be in bed. You're ill. Look at your bare feet. You'll catch your death.

Her voice is dull, lacks conviction.

– I couldn't sleep, I tell her: I wanted to come downstairs.

I seat myself opposite her, on the other side of the range, removing my feet from the solid cold of the floor and tucking them up underneath me, pulling my nightgown over my toes to cover them.

The air between us is difficult and ugly. Yesterday we had the shouting and crying, the recriminations. You wicked girl a married man immoral filth. I could not defend myself. Today she is exhausted. I have hurt her. Broken her. She slumps, her head beaten forwards, belly slack under her apron, and she does not want to look at me. I disgust her too much.

William's hand grips my elbow, keeps me moving forward across the street. The Salpetrière looms in front of us, big as Buckingham Palace. The entrance hall and the corridor we are shown down are carpeted, warm, smell of soap and beeswax. I worry about my boots stained with seawater, grey tidemarks on the black leather; no time to polish them before we left the hotel. William squeezes my arm: Dr Charcot won't mind. In the doctor's big office, full of bookcases and tables covered with books, I perch on one end of a leather sofa, while the men stand together at the other end of the room, talking in French, a rapid mutter. Sweat squirms in the palms of my hands, greasy, dampens my gloves.

I study the pictures on the wall next to me. Peering close, I see they are photographs, all three of the same young girl. She wears a rough white robe, a sort of nightgown, that shows a lot of her neck and arms. She's inside a cot with bars. In the first picture she sits up in bed, her arms raised in supplication, her hands clasped in prayer, her long black hair tumbling down her back and her eyes rolling backwards to show the whites. In the second, she cocks her head to one side, her arms raised in astonishment and a sort of pleasure, one leg crossed over the other, her nightgown thrown back from her thighs, fallen open across her breasts, her teeth bared in a fixed grin. In the third, she is flung back on her pillows, her hands crossed over her half-exposed breast, her eyes closed in rapture, her mouth curved into a strange smile.

In my room back at the hotel, there is a picture like these: a half-naked woman with long loose hair that doesn't quite cover her bare breasts, one hand clutching the sheet wound round her waist, the other holding a skull. William said she was a French saint. He was impatient, no time for explanations, he wanted to get me out of the door and into the waiting cab.

William has taken many photographs of me during our seances together. Evidence that Hattie exists, and walks around his study while I lie in trance on the sofa in the library. Only Hattie doesn't like to stand still, as you have to do for five minutes while the camera works. She comes out as a blur, because she moves too much. So William takes a second set, using me as the model for Hattie. Just to record her gestures. He places me in different positions, lifting my arms, adjusting my leg, tipping up my chin with his finger. He puts me in the attitudes he says Hattie strikes. He opens the front of Hattie's robe to show her breasts, flicking the nipples to stiffen them. Hattie's hands grasp the front of her robe and tear it open to show her breasts. He lays Hattie on the rug in front of the fire, her knees apart, her robe rucked up over them to show her plump white thighs, the golden tuft at the top. Hattie falls back onto the rug in front of the fire, not caring that her gown is rucked up anyhow, showing her legs. Hattie is shameless, because she is a spirit. William says there is no need to be ashamed. Flora copies what Hattie does, to help with the experiments. William puts his fingers inside Hattie, while Flora lies unconscious on the sofa next door. Hattie is frightened at first, she wriggles and whimpers and says no. William says hush, it's all right, be a good girl now, don't cry. Remember your promise not to tell. Remember the money. Remember I've promised to help you. William is a doctor, so it's all right. It's science, it's an experiment. He puts his hand over Hattie's mouth, blotting her no. Her body strains upwards against his, saying yes, no, I'm a good girl daddy. She only lets him because he's a doctor. He's feeling inside her because he needs to know how real Hattie is, what her responses are to stimulation of different sorts. Hattie helps him. She opens. She can't help it. His voice is soothing, calm, he stays in control, while his fingers explore her wetness, her soft ribbed insides, harder, harder. Stay still, don't move so much. It's just a medical examination, his cool fingers reaching deeper in, deeper, harder, she lifts, she rises, she moans, she collapses. On the sofa next door, Flora whimpers in her trance. Hattie's not a virgin anyway, William discovers that, she's a bad girl, she's shameless. There's no need to be ashamed. William sits beside Flora on the sofa and takes her pulse, holds her hand in his. Good girl, Flora, well done. Flora knows nothing. Flora would never do what Hattie does. Flora is a good girl.

I sit on the leather sofa in Dr Charcot's office, my hands clasped in my lap, my ankles pressed together. The men have fallen silent. I see them looking at me looking at the photographs of the young girl in the white nightdress.

My mother's face, when finally she lifts her head and looks at me, is bewildered, bitter.

– Whatever shall we do with you. What have I done to deserve this. Do you realize what you've done.

I'm shivering with cold. No shawl, my nightdress no protection against the draughts cutting in under the kitchen door. My face burns, my back freezes, my hands are red lumps of cold meat. Sourness clots in my stomach, rises up through my throat, onto my tongue, bursts from between my lips.

– You never wanted me anyway. You didn't want me to be born. Don't think I don't remember you telling me, because I do.

She swells up opposite, a red balloon I will pierce. Her face in red shreds.

– You told me the day of Father's funeral. Don't you remember? I do. You tried to get rid of me over and over. That's what you told me. You didn't want me to be born. You tried your best to kill me.

Dr Charcot is escorting me to the lecture theatre. He bows, I place my fingertips on his proffered arm, we glide out of his office, down the corridor. I walk with delicate steps, my head held high but my eyes lowered. My skirt swishes on the floor behind me.

The theatre is hidden in the heart of the hospital behind locked doors. It is here, William explains to me, that Dr Charcot lectures to his medical students and teaches them how to treat the patients. It is here that the patients come each week, to show the students how ill they are and how much they need treatment.

Sometimes a select public audience is invited, for there is much to see and learn. Today it is just the doctors and the students.

The theatre is small and deep, close tiers of seats packed steeply, rising in a stack of half-circles to the ceiling. No windows, the light coming from groups of gas jets on the walls that hiss and splutter and smell acrid, mixing with the perfume of hair oil and polish and some sweet, sickly odour I have no name for. The theatre stoops over the small raised dais on which Dr Charcot stands, hands thrust into his waistcoat pockets. I have been handed to a seat in the front row. I am the only woman in the audience.

In the yellow light I stare at the brown varnished arm of my chair, then, bolder, at the oil painting behind the dais. It's a picture of this theatre. There are the students, rapt dolls, in their seats; there are the stout bearded doctors in frockcoats; there are the stiff nurses in blue dresses; there is Dr Charcot himself, holding a half-naked girl in his arms. I'm not in the picture, of course. I can't see myself. The girl with half her clothes torn off looks rather like the one in the photograph in his office. She's wearing a white nightgown open all down the front and her mouth is jerked into a grin.

I'm waiting, with the rest of the audience, hushed in the yellow gloom, for the performance to begin in a blaze of lights. I don't know what play it will be, of course. No one's given me a programme. And I don't suppose I shall understand the French. When Dr Charcot starts to speak, William whispers to me that it's all technical medical details, too complicated to translate. I understand one word. It recurs often enough for me to grasp it, turn it over in my hand. *Isterry*. History? And then *famm*. History and women?

The women patients are putting on a play: the history of a woman. One after another comes forward through the double doors at the back of the stage, in the grip of a blue-uniformed nurse. Dr Charcot welcomes each one affectionately, puts her into an armchair on the dais, soothes her nervousness by passing his hands gently to and fro in front of her face. Then he makes a different gesture, like a command, and each actress in turn springs up from her chair, throws herself without hesitation into her role.

Dr Charcot is a ringmaster: the first woman drops on all fours, sniffs the legs of her chair, waggles her rump, barks.

Dr Charcot is a magician: the second woman takes the top hat he offers her, cradles it in her arms, rocks it to and fro as she walks up and down the dais and croons to it.

Dr Charcot is God: the third woman hops on one leg, arms outstretched, squawks, tries to fly.

Dr Charcot is a great artist: the fourth woman accepts the piece of charcoal he gives her and begins to eat it, drooling with pleasure.

Behind me the men discreetly gasp, laugh. Beside me, William stares at the stage. But he hasn't forgotten me: knowing tension is rising out of me like steam, he pats my arm with a slow stroke, takes my hand in his, clasps it. And his touch, as always, calms me, slackens the thump of my heartbeat, makes my muscles relax. It is the same thing that Dr Charcot knows how to do to his patients, a message passed in silence through flesh, from William to me; an instruction. It is the same thing I learned with Rosina, with Mr Potson, with Minny: how to receive the thought of the other, from hand to hand, wishes and commands translated, the morse code of the body. Lulled, I do not resist when William nips my elbow, pulls me up and forward, onto my feet. I watch Miss Milk step onto the dais and seat herself opposite Professor Preston, Dr Charcot standing just behind her chair.

My mother rises, seizes the blue-checked cloth, twists her hands in it, pulls it tight. But she can't strangle her words. They squeeze out of her, cold water.

– You're a wicked girl to remind me of anything I said that day. When I was half-demented with grief.

– My father, I begin.

She spits the words out, bits of dead flesh and bone.

– Your father. It was your father who wanted me to get rid of you. He went on and on at me about it. It was he who didn't want you, not me. Funny how you don't remember me telling you that.

Terror wants to be wax plugging my ears. Too late. I've heard her bitter truth. Her sour milk truth. She looms over me, clutching the blue cloth, gabbling.

– I told you. I told you that day, going to the funeral. You remember as well as I do, only you pretend you don't, you little liar. He never wanted to marry me. He told me to get rid of the baby. So I tried. But I couldn't manage it. I tried everything I could think of. He was so angry with me. He said I hadn't tried enough. He said I forced him to marry me.

The blue cloth she's trying to tear in two is intact, but her face isn't. It crumples, it splits, as her pain bursts out, red and wet.

– He only married me because he had to. Because you were on the way. And look at the way you've turned out. A bad lot, you are. He was right. It was better you should never have been born. He wanted you dead. You're so bad. You'll be the death of me.

She weeps into the cloth. I don't weep. I'm made of black iron, I'm the stove, and the fire inside me has gone out, I'm cold black ashes at the bottom of the grate. Too cold and heavy to move. It's mother who moves, out of the door and up the stairs. Her footsteps drum on the treads like rain on the roof of a funeral carriage. The blue cloth lies on the floor, a crumpled rag. I lean down from my chair, pick it up and spread it over my face. So that I can make myself go away.

The play I'm going to act with William will be different from the ones we've done before. Hattie isn't here, because it's not a proper seance. Her absence is a hollow sharply carved inside me. Apprehension seeps in, begins to fill me. If Hattie's not here with me, I can't slide into unconsciousness, can't depend on her to do the talking. Then it strikes me that she's like a daughter: I've given birth to her, she's grown up and left me. I mustn't plead with her to come back. I must act on my own. I'm pleased with this thought, and want to tell William about it, but now is not the time. He is leaning forward, explaining what we are going to do. His voice drones. I'm excited, don't want to listen, it will be all right, I want to tell him. He is holding my hands lightly in his and telling me about a new sort of experiment. Hypnosis he calls it. What Dr Charcot did with the other women patients. With the women patients. That's not true, I want to tell him: that was the circus, couldn't you see? But he doesn't want me to interrupt. He doesn't want me to speak. He wants me to mime, and the doctors and students will do the guessing. We're going to play charades.

I'm patient with him as he rambles on, explaining. Dear William, so anxious that I should understand, that I should not be nervous. I wait, smiling, for him to finish. I'm clear, light, ready. I'm brimming with words, with love, ideas. If I may only convey them in dumb-show, then I'm content. William's so proud of me. I shan't let him down. For the first time I'm going to show him who Flora is. Hattie's not here, and so Flora must act. He thinks Flora is just a little girl. He thinks Hattie's the wise grown-up one, the only one who knows. I'll surprise him.

If the daughter were out of the way, then the mother and father would be able to love each other truly, without restraint. I know that. So I take my hands out of William's, I snatch my eyes away from his, and I rise from my chair. I advance to the footlights, and salute my audience: the men haloed in yellow gaslight. Their white faces swim in the darkness, their white knuckles rest on the desks, curve upon curve of bits of white bone, of white moons. I turn back and take up my place in the centre of the stage with my fellow actors: the woman in a stiff blue dress, the handsome man in the armchair.

Since I may not speak, and so betray the secret words my watchers want to guess, I must let my body shape words for me. My body full of knowledge. I can't speak French, and my audience doesn't understand English, so I must act my meaning through my body. I understand the necessity. It would be easier just to tell William, and let him translate my words into French, but Dr Charcot doesn't want that. He wants me to do it all by myself. He wants to see how well I can mime, how well I can hide my meaning while at the same time revealing it.

It's difficult to show them all who Flora is without using any words. So I copy some of the gestures of the girl in the white nightdress in the photographs. She is well-rehearsed, and, following her movements, so am I.

Flora is the little girl in the white nightdress who sits on her father's knee. He tickles her and she tickles him back. She laughs so much she is almost sick. Flora twirls and dances for her daddy. Naughty little flirt, he calls her, laughing: pretty little coquette. Mother is cross: don't teach her such tricks, what good will come of it? Mother is jealous of Flora, of her golden curls and dimples. Mother is ugly. She has no time to play with Daddy like Flora does. Daddy loves Flora best. They love each other so much. Mother is old. Flora is frightened she will die. Flora stands in the kitchen doorway, watching her mother cry, head laid on her hands on the table. Flora dances for Dr Charcot and for William just like she dances for her daddy.

A cruel woman in a blue dress and veil bends over Flora, pretending to take her pulse. In a moment she will tear off her veil and press it over Flora's face until she suffocates and can be put away in the oak cupboard in the kitchen. Flora jerks from side to side to avoid this and the cruel woman retreats. Flora dances for her daddy again. She must trick the cruel woman into

127

believing they are friends; she must smile at her, charm her, listen to her. The cruel woman is too stupid to see that under her very nose she is being made a fool of. Mincing Minny. Daddy would like to get rid of her but can't say so. Flora understands him without any words. At night she creeps into his bed while the cruel woman sleeps and snuggles up to him. She's his little bear, he tells her: his little cat. She lies between the man and woman in their bed. She protects her daddy from the stupid cruel woman. She is the sword that keeps them apart and keeps them chaste. She is her father's sword. She belongs to him. One night she dreams that thus she can go where he goes: into the warm sweet mother.

Alone in the kitchen, curled in my chair, the blue cloth covering my face, I abandon myself to the cold creeping through me, wanting to die. But tears keep me alive; I can't freeze; I keep on melting. Admit it, admit it, my tears insist: you wished your mother dead. You wanted her out of the way. You wanted her killed.

Mother's right. I'm a wicked girl. Nothing else to say.

There is something I want to say but I mustn't say it. To speak would be to break my promise to William and Dr Charcot. It's safer not to speak. That way the men will love me. If I don't tell them how I feel. I'm not a fool. I know they want the pretty medium entranced, not Hattie's power, not Flora's rage. Even Hattie tends to say only what she knows the men can cope with hearing. She makes a translation, to what they can bear. She's not a fool either. She keeps the secret, that Flora is angry. She doesn't tell.

I am the girl in the white nightgown in the photograph. We undress for the doctors; slow ritual we have rehearsed so often. Their eyes examine us. They think they have guessed our secret thoughts. How can they? We don't speak. We just dance for them, which is all they want. They are delighted with our performance. Delighted daddies, their darlings on their knees. I'm on my knees, in front of Daddy. He doesn't know I know he wanted me dead. He mustn't guess. Better to stop here, on my knees.

William wakes me from my dream, stroking me with a voice smooth as chocolate. I lift my head obediently. I'm his trained poodle. Good Flora. There's a good girl. Sit down nicely, now. Good Flora. He's passing his hands to and fro in the air in front of my face. I'm still a long way off, but I see his grimace at Dr Charcot, a private significant smile.

I know what's happened. Also I don't know what's happened. I've got to be very careful. The floor of the grey stone corridor is so slippery, my feet want to skate away on it and leave my body behind. My head wants to twist round on my neck like a spinning top, sever itself, bowl over the cold flags after my dirty boots. I want to give myself away, get rid of these hands, this sick stomach, this pumping heart. I've given myself away to the doctor. That was silly of me. Also dangerous. I need to recover myself now and get out of here.

I'm on the leather sofa in Dr Charcot's office. He and William stand between me and the door, talking. Occasional words detach themselves from sentences and float free in the half-dark, bumping into the furniture. *Isterry. Delloosyon.* I catch the words as they drift past me and squeeze them to death in my hands, then I stow them in my pocket, where they can do no harm. Later I'll take them out and have a good look at them.

When the two men turn the white glare of their attention on me, I decide to sit up. I throw off my shawl of faintness, I take a deep breath to sober myself. Dr Charcot polishes his beard with one hand as he speaks, rests the other on his swollen grey waistcoat. You can smile at insects spreadeagled under your poised boot, and that's how he smiles at me. Mother would say I've made a disgusting exhibition of myself and she'd be right. William agrees with Mother; his face is sulky, cold, though he tries to sound friendly.

William says that since I'm still feeling so weak it would be more sensible to stay in the hospital overnight under the eye of a doctor. They'll give me a nice room, a nice supper, a nurse to take care of me. He's responsible for me while we're here; he can't have me wandering round Paris and fainting all over the place, now can he? And in any case Dr Charcot has been so impressed by my performance in the theatre just now that he'd be only too happy to take another look at me in the morning. We'll all go to the theatre again together.

William's voice is hearty and false. It's the same voice he uses to Minny when barring her from our evening seances. Minny and I are his children, fragile, to be coaxed into sensible behaviour. How much Minny must hate me for what I've done to her. I recognize that, for the first time.

Minny's hatred pushes my head round to look at the photographs again. The mad girl in white. But she's not mad, she's angry. She lowers her arms from their posture of supplication, she clenches her teeth then shouts out, her hands are fists striking the air sweet with drugs. She leaps from her cot, through the heavy black bars that frame her and try to hold her still, she smashes through the glass of the photograph and bounds to the floor. For a moment she stands in front of me, trembling and bewildered, looking into my face.

It's Hattie. She's come back to me, because I need her so badly. But she doesn't recognize me. And she doesn't want me to stay here. She sucks on a bleeding knuckle, she shakes shards of glass from her white robe, she glances from me to the men. She's frightened they're going to lock her up in the dark again. Hitching the loose top of her nightgown back up over her shoulder, she makes for the door.

She's showing me the way out. She's leaving me. I mustn't let her out of my sight. Hurling myself to my feet, I push past William and Dr Charcot and throw myself at the door. Through it, and down the corridor. Hattie is just ahead, a white streamer, she tugs me onwards, I put out my hands to catch her but can't, I must follow her. She's my white rope, I whip myself forward, the men will try to catch me and I must catch Hattie. She leads me out. She delivers me, into the sunshine, into the colours and noise of the street. Then she vanishes.

I return from Paris, as I came to it, alone. William is finished with me. His researches into me are finished. My black dress holds me up. My boots walk me along the station platform, onto the boat. My gloves knock on the door of my mother's house.

William denies he ever touched me. He says I am imagining it because I am ill. Even to imagine it shows how wicked I am. He says that all the time I lay entranced upon the sofa in his house he stayed on the other side of the blue curtain. That blue veil separated us. It was Hattie who walked about and spoke with him, not Flora. If I deny that then I am nothing but a hysteric who suffers from delusions. I am a wicked girl to make up such stories.

Mother believes my story. She says I am a wicked girl. She makes a lot of noise. Then she sends me to bed because I am ill.

I am bad ugly cruel stupid. I know that much. I want, I don't know what I want. To vanish, to disappear. But I can't. I'm too big and solid with sadness. There's no excuse for what I've done. I hold the knowledge of it in my arms.

I haul myself from my chair and leave the kitchen, to return to bed. I don't want Rosina to find me here when she comes back from wherever she's gone; I don't want to have to face her. On the landing outside my room I pause in the blue oblong under the window. Perhaps if I stay here in the blue light it will dissolve me, wash me away. So I sit down on the stairs.

My only companion is the cold white wall next to me. I lay my head against it.

If the wall were soft, and warm. If the wall breathed steadily, in and out. If Hattie were the wall. If Hattie were the house. If her strong body could comfort and sustain me, hold me. If her walls were strong enough to hold me up and hold my pain. If the house could stoop over me, console me, mourn with me.

I wall up my pain in the house, on the landing under the window with its bit of blue glass. I put all my pain and grief into the wall, sealing it up hard and smooth as ice, and I leave it there.

I read with sorrow, dearest Mamma, your missive explaining that a visit to London on your part is at the moment out of the question. We must defer it until the New Year, that is all. How overjoyed the children will be to see you after such a long interval! Already we have begun to plan all sorts of outings and excitements. That we must delay a little our pleasure at seeing you is perhaps no bad thing; by the end of the year, I am convinced, I shall have completely vanquished this silly indisposition of mine.

I must curtail my longing to write to you at my usual length. Dr Felton decrees that my brain is at present over-stimulated, and that the exercise of all my mental and intellectual faculties must be prevented for the moment. The regime he now prescribes is an intensification of the former one: in addition to total bed rest in a darkened room, frequent nourishing meals, and the drinking of copious quantities of warm milk, I am also to desist from all reading of books and all writing of letters. I am in his hands, of course, so I do not complain. I am sure it is all for the best. I am too drowsy to scribble more, and, in any case, I dare not displease my careful physician by disobeying his orders. William writes cheerfully from Paris that all is well, so I need have no worries on that score.

Ever your loving daughter,
Minny.

Death should not be frightening. If the proper rituals are observed, the proper precautions taken, then the dead Queen will live on happily amongst her ancestors. She is mighty; she roams the over-arching sky and the underworld; she joins the celestial hunt and is drawn across the dark clouds of night on a glittering barge. She is cut loose from earth; a spirit who roams as she pleases between stars and moon; yet if she wishes to return to earth and re-visit the land of her fathers there is a way back. The stone door, called the false door, that joins the spirit world in which she now moves to her deep tomb in the rock. Going back there is like being born; she crawls through a tunnel of air; she beats with her fists on the door until it swings open and deposits her back inside the vaulted chamber cradling her sarcophagus. There inside its several wood and linen skins her body lies, intact, beautiful, incorrupt, swathed in bandages, a newborn's swaddling bands. There are the pottery models of bread, meat and beer, the model servants, the model furniture. There is the real treasure. There are the real signs painted on the wall which promise her eternal life.

Such is the teaching on which I was brought up, and which has consoled me throughout all the difficulties and dangers of my reign. Peace will come. I shall see my father again.

Yet in my dream last night such is not the case.

When I swoop down through the darkness to re-enter my sepulchre and feast my eyes on its kingly splendours the air is made of spears and holds me back. The air resists and laughs at me. The air weaves a web of spikes across the entrance to my tomb and will not let me pass. On the walls, all the painted scenes depicting the triumphs of my life have been washed over. Over the doorway, the writing reciting prayers for me has been defaced, half obliterated. On the columns, all the cartouches containing the hieroglyphs spelling out my name have been savagely hacked out.

I have been unwritten. Written out. Written off. Therefore I am not even dead. I never was. I am non-existent. There is no I.

I was a man and a pharaoh and a king. I was mighty because I was male and bore the sacred sign of maleness and of kingship. Now that my name has been hacked off the walls and columns of my tomb the sign of my kingship has been broken off me.

I am lacking. I am a lack. I am nothing but a poor dead body that lacks the sign of life: I am female.

No. I can't say it. I can't bear to say it.

I am a spirit condemned to roam for ever through the dark, never to find a resting place, never to be venerated again as a god on earth. I have lost the great male force that was once in me. I have lost the title of Pharaoh. I have lost the carved and painted house that sheltered my remains.

I am an exile, doomed to wander in the night, homeless, searching for something I shall never find.

When I wake from this dream my room seems dank and cold, too dark. I shout for a servant. I want someone to come and comfort me, just as when I'm a child and wake from nightmares shouting for my nurse and for a light. For the moment no one hears me and I remain alone.

What if the dream were an omen? What if it were true?

I shall seek for a scribe who will write down my name and let me live again. I shall dart forwards through hundreds of years, searching for a faithful scribe who will spell me right and let me rise. One whose hand will dance to my spelling.

Yesterday I went to visit Sister Julian for the first time in years. I've been expecting you, she said in her letter welcoming my proposed visit: I had a feeling you would come.

She had changed, and so had the convent. The visitors' parlour was now called the common room. Gone was the speckled brown wallpaper with its embossed border, gone the carved sideboard and stiff chairs with tapestry seats ranged along the wall, gone was the big oval table draped with a green chenille cloth and set with a bunch of dried palms in a red glass vase and a statue of the

Virgin with wire stars around her head, gone were the Victorian pictures of pallid saints, the framed photograph of the Foundress in round spectacles. Gone was the smell of polish and candles, holy cleanliness, gone the comfortable gloom. That bit of history had been cut out of the convent and thrown away. In its place was a modern box lit by dangling fluorescent tubes, dotted with groups of easy chairs in shiny pine with orange cushions. The parquet floor was hidden under thin cotton rugs, and the walls, flowered in beige and tangerine, were hung with posters, cheery and sentimental, doves of peace and the like.

Sister Julian grimaced at me.

– I don't like it either.

She bit into a plump white marmite sandwich. Never before had I seen a nun eat. Now I was surrounded by nuns entertaining their friends, gossiping over cups of tea poured from the urn on a trolley in one corner. It was hard to tell the nuns from the other women, now that they were in ordinary clothes. I was glad that Sister Julian did not request me to call her Dorothy, which she told me was her baptismal name, and I was glad to see she wore a compromise habit still, a long blue dress and a blue scarf knotted at the back of her head. It suited her, far better than the grey crimplene overalls and veils she wore before. I looked at her white hair, her mottled hands, the shapeless ankles that bulged over her smart black suede lace-ups. An old lady.

Most of the younger nuns, she told me, had moved out, to take jobs and live in bedsits amongst the local people, and their now unused dormitories had been converted into a hostel for homeless girls. The motherhouse in Rouen had done the same.

– No more Mother Superiors either, Sister Julian said: we're all plain Sister now. You should hear those young ones talk. No respect.

A change from the old days, when the convent took in single Catholic ladies fallen on hard times, gave them bedsits in return for their labour as teachers. I remembered Miss Glenny, with her sausage-curled blonde wig, knee-length elastic stockings and bad smell, who was mad, and taught us geography; thin Miss Dunn and her fat sister, blind Miss Katy who taught us singing and piano and eurythmic dancing; Miss Jost with her rosetted shoes and loose hair and linen smocks who taught us art and was sacked when her belly got too big.

I thought further back. Seven years old. The black and white chequered floor of the entrance hall. Outside, the square guarded by wrought iron spears, ornamental cherry trees sprouting over their thick black tips, an enormous sycamore presiding over a sweep of green turf. I wanted to collect fallen sprays of blossom from the gutter clotted with pollen dust and pink petals, but my aunt tugged me inside to where the sun was shut out and it smelt like church. That floor like a chessboard, slippery. If I didn't step on the cracks I'd be all right. A tall black chess-piece with no feet or hair glided towards us and detached me from my aunt's woollen hand.

– The youngest boarder we'd ever had, Sister Julian said, picking up my thought: but you didn't cry. Everyone spoiled you to death. You were the darling of the house, a spoilt little princess. Of course your mother and aunt having been pupils here, we wanted to do all we could to help.

I remembered the calm of that house at dusk, the utter hush when all the daygirls had gone home and the corridors and landings filled with shadows. The wide staircase rose up from the hall and circled floor after floor. A statue at each turn of the stairs, saints I prayed to as I passed in case the burglar waited for me under my bed in the dark. In the cramped semi where I lived with my aunt and uncle and three cousins and had to sleep on the fold-down settee in the living room, I knew that the burglar could only arrive through the front hall. The nuns' house was so big he could be hiding anywhere. So, to be safe, I became the burglar. Night after night I crept up the stairs towards the dormitory getting my slippered shuffle just right, whispering urgently to myself to hush, to be a good girl now.

– You didn't seem to miss your uncle and aunt at all, Sister Julian went on: you never mentioned them. You seemed quite happy. And you turned out so well, despite everything.

I said nothing at the age of seven because there was nothing to say. My aunt took my words with her when she went away and left me. She left me because I was bad. I was left with badness. At night, in my narrow white bed encircled by white curtains, I escaped into another country called Egypt where I was king.

– You remember those stories you used to make up? Sister Julian asked: whatever trouble you got into, you always had a story ready for getting out of it. You were such a wonderful liar, I was almost sorry I had to punish you so often. But it was a sin of course. It had to be punished.

I was lucky, the nuns told me, not to have been taken into care after my mother left me in my basket at my aunt's and ran away to Australia to forget her sin and find a husband. I was lucky, the nuns told me, that my aunt and uncle took me in. I thought I was lucky to have found a home full of mothers in black. I was lucky they didn't let men in. In that house of chaste women there was no room for a truth that included uncles.

At night, everyone in the convent had to observe the Great Silence. Only to God could we talk in the dark.

I couldn't see my uncle, because it was so dark. I tried to pretend that he was just a voice, like on the telephone, the one that squatted next to my bed-settee in the sitting room.

The voice whispered that it was our little secret. I was to tell no one, certainly not my aunt, she wasn't to be upset because she was having another baby. If I told I would be sent away and never see her again. I did as he said, and told no one. He went on whispering to me in the dark, night after night. I didn't dare to stop him. I was wicked not to. He was only a telephone. In the end I was sent away. My aunt found me too much to cope with, along with the new baby, and got the convent to take me in. I spent my holidays there, refusing to go back to what the nuns called my home. My aunt didn't mind. After a while she stopped coming to visit me, and I was glad. My uncle's hands were no longer in my bed at night, and so I could stop thinking about him. Until I bought my house and the phone calls started.

– The one thing you refused to learn, Sister Julian said, crooking her little finger over her teacup: was a regard for the truth.

I kissed her goodbye, briefly holding her plump soft body in my arms. She was small. She seemed very old.

I did try to tell the chaplain about it once. At my first confession at the age of eight, when I was being prepared for my first Holy Communion. I'd practised beforehand with Sister Julian, so that I'd know what to do. The chaplain was red-faced and told incomprehensible jokes. He was supposed to represent God, but to me God was female, invisible, and black: God dwelt in the nuns' dark cloister that we were forbidden to enter, God lurked behind the black-curtained grille separating off the nuns' chapel from the main nave where we knelt for Mass and Benediction, God was hidden in the nuns' hearts under the black capes they wore to go to church and sing. The chaplain couldn't understand what I was trying to confess. I couldn't get the words out. He waited, patiently, on the other side of the metal grille. I knelt on the hard prie-dieu, hearing my voice fail. The confessional was like a little cupboard, musty and dark, with a purple curtain at my back that smelled of incense and mothballs. I gripped my new rosary, pale blue beads on a silver chain with a dangling silver crucifix. I confessed to stealing lumps of sugar from the kitchen. Be off with you now, he rapped: and say three Hail Marys. He gabbled my absolution and I fled. For years I took Christ's body into my mouth knowing I was full of sin. I lost my faith deliberately when I left school, hoping that that way I'd lose my sinfulness too. Years later I took many men's bodies into mine, and felt nothing. Sitting in the confessional in the *abbaye* at Fécamp, some sort of a God returned to me, one who demands to be known through the work of my hands that can destroy, repair, create.

Most nights now I dream of my uncle. I haven't seen him for almost thirty years, yet he comes back to me because we have work still to do together. He's not a faceless whisper in the dark. He shuffles in his leather slippers. He wears his vest and pyjama trousers, his old plaid dressing-gown. We stand under the high vaulted roof of the underground basement kitchen, lapped by the red glow of flames. The incorrupt body of the Foundress lies in its glass coffin under the kitchen table. I shall say Mass on top of it. Sister Bridget swings a sauceboat, Sœur Marie-Madeleine stokes the fire, Sister Julian holds a white linen towel. My uncle lies on the kitchen table. He is the body, and he is the blood. I sort his dismembered limbs. Bit by bit I feed him into the red fire in the range. My task is to purify him. I have to burn him, to burn off the monstrous bits he doesn't need, the growths that disfigure him: his second pair of hands, his second mouth and tongue, his second penis. The fire divests him of these, one by one. Then I rake out the coals, to cool the fire, and my uncle lies naked in the ashes with the right number of limbs, newborn.

Each time I wake from this dream I am punched by pain. I wait till you've gone downstairs to the studio to paint, then I let myself cry, sobs that tear through me. It's my work. There is a lot of it to do.

The old man turned up punctually this morning, at nine. His voice was hesitant and polite as usual. I apologized for my rudeness on the telephone all these weeks. I said I'd been very ill and just couldn't bear talking to strangers. His face was irritable and pink. He wore a navy blazer with gilt buttons, smooth tubes of grey terylene trousers, a red and blue striped tie. He didn't look at all like my uncle. I'd got the two boxes out of the attic behind the bed in our room and lugged them down to the sitting room in preparation for his coming. No dead body in the attic after all; just boxes overlooked by Miss Cotter's relatives when they cleared the house.

Cardboard boxes grimy with dust, sealed with brown masking tape. He tore back the tops to check the contents. I peered over his shoulder.

The first one was full of old children's books. He lifted out a couple and looked at them, then put them back.

The second box contained a pile of old photograph albums bound in red half-calf. Tissue paper between the leaves, faded brown silk markers. Frizzy-haired beauties in starched blouses and boaters, fat pasty babies in frocks, scowling matrons in black tents, young men with moustaches striking jokey poses. Images fading fast on glossy pasteboard. Underneath, the legends in neat brown copperplate: on the beach at Southend; Flora puts her hair up; Rosina's wedding day. The old man slapped the album shut when he saw how interested I was.

– Family souvenirs. Mustn't touch. They're very precious.

Tucked down the side were several stiff exercise books beautifully bound in brown paper. I squinted at the writing on the cover of the one nearest to me. Roman capitals, black and well-spaced. Something about milk. Then the old man closed the box and picked it up.

He wouldn't stay for a cup of tea. He drove off with his boxes, still cross with me. I couldn't blame him after the way I'd treated him on the telephone. And the state of the house, still so unfinished, clearly shocked him. Crazy hippy, his eyes said: slut.

I was restless. I prowled about the hall, stroking the banisters you've been stripping, checking the heap of post and circulars on the windowsill. I thought about clearing up the rest of the little attic, full of other rubbish left from the old lady's time. I got as far as the top landing before I realized how tired and lazy I felt. I stood in the blue light from the landing window, I checked the fresh putty you've put in the window-frame to secure the ancient glass and its four oblongs of brave colour, I looked at the wall there that so badly needs re-plastering and re-painting. I thought:

it can wait. I made a cup of tea and came in here to scribble, to put my feet up for half an hour, to clasp my hands gently over you, baby, dancer in your warm house of stretched skin. When you beat the drum of me I shall call back to you. Many weeks to wait before your birth. No way of knowing whether you'll stay inside me that long.

George and I marry with little fuss. Mother's there with Aunt Dolly, George's parents and brothers, and Rosina and the little ones. Afterwards at home we have oysters, plentiful and fresh, tasting of the sea and of lemon, as many as we can eat. Also there are crab patties on a yellow dish, a bowl of watercress, boiled gammon, a jug of celery, cheesecakes on lace doyleys. The tablecloth is white, glossy with starch. Mother's brought out her best plates, the ones with ivy leaves round the rims. George's father mixes a jug of champagne and Guinness. I remember Aunt Dolly playing the piano, and the little ones lining up in their sailor-suits in order of size, hands on the shoulders of the one in front, then marching gravely round the room while Mother beats time with a spoon.

It's as clear to me now as it was then: George in his new check trousers with his black hair sleeked back and his coat tightly buttoned high on his chest, me in my blue costume with brown velvet trimmings and real silk cornflowers in my hat. Suddenly faint, and heaving. George steers me to the lavatory outside. Holding my head so tenderly between his hands as I retch over the bowl, the door propped open letting in sunlight and air, tendrils of green against the little window, a bar of sunlight on the wall behind the china handle of the flush. I cut up my wedding photographs and threw them away when George died. Lily was furious: Mother, what right have you to do that? I didn't care what she thought. My grief eased itself a little through jabbing at grey shiny cardboard, ripping my mouth in two, crushing George's face between my hands. He was my lover; Lily didn't understand that.

George and I stay on at Clarence Road because it's cheaper than lodgings and we need to save money. My old bedroom is unchanged, except that now there's a man in it, his shirts in the chest of drawers and his boots under the washstand.

Mother plumps up for him like a cushion. A man to look after again. She cooks him the food he likes: suet puddings, steak and kidney pies, mutton chops with lots of gravy, treacle tarts. She listens for his whistle as he runs up the front steps, then lumbers up to make his tea. For him she unbends, laughing when he teases her, always looking for him first when she comes through the door; his presence warms her, loosens her. At night he paces the kitchen with Lily over his shoulder while she sews. I watch them. In our room he's mine. The coverlet on our bed is pink satin, with a raised pattern done in quilting. I have it still. Even now I wake up and look for his head sunk in the pillow next to mine. Still in my dreams I rage for him, stumbling after him: lover, where have you gone?

Rosina's long since gone. Immediately after the wedding she departs. She goes into lodgings at the dressmaker's. Soon after that she gets her revenge all right. Sometimes Mother tries to speak of her, to excuse her, but I won't listen.

George knows I am not good, but he loves me. He is like my father was: gentle, wanting to hurt no one, wanting to please. He's so tender with us women who love him. Like my father did, he takes it as his due. Like my father too in not wanting to get married young, but then settling down all right once the baby's arrived.

As soon as I've weaned Lily I go on a tour of the Midlands, taking George with me as my manager and leaving Lily with my mother. Now it's George who's my assistant, who shares all the secrets of my trade. My little sister's gone. It's George who helps me dress for my first appearance, at the Temperance Hall in Leicester, it's George who holds my hand as we wait in the wings of the little platform, crammed up against a stack of banners, the dust on their twisted gold cords brushing our noses and making us sneeze. It's George who understands I'm worried the spirits won't come back after the bad things I did before I was married. It's George I look for as I come off stage later that afternoon. That night in our lodgings he produces a bottle of champagne, a waxed paper parcel of cold roast chicken, a paper cone of gherkins and capers. We feast, huddled up together in the double bed, laughing at the landlady's hideous china ornaments and temperance texts. It's raining outside, George licks the grease off my chin.

Ten years later I've saved enough to buy the house in Clarence Road off the landlord, and we have a son, Jo. With the lodgers gone, we've got a proper parlour at last. In the afternoons I hold private seances there, and at night use it for doing our accounts. Every stick of new furniture is paid for by me.

One night George comes in having taken a chill. It goes to his lungs. A week later he is dead.

It hurts writing this. I was fooling myself when I wrote down at the start, all those months ago, that I was doing it for fun, to amuse myself. I think I'm doing it to bring George back to me, to make Jo live again, to pick up my son's poor shattered body and mend it, to hold my husband in my arms and heal him. But I only get as far as feeling my sorrow all over again. A son should not die before his mother. Jo's death is a great gaping hole inside me. I'm his grave; empty; his body isn't in me. Only in dreams does he come back, staring at me from sightless sockets filled with blood.

Never once have I been able to contact Jo in the course of a seance. The others always get there first, regiments of young men calling out from the mud in which they lay dead and unburied and alone. Jo let them go first as he always did. Even in death he hung back and let the other ghosts reach his mother first. The young men told me about their manner of dying, their manner of surviving in the trenches before they went into battle. I softened their accounts for my listeners' sakes, the wives mothers sisters sweethearts who came to me imploring my help. I could bear what the young men told me, but I did not think their loved ones could. I bore it for them. I lied to them. Harry and Johnny are at peace, I said: they suffer no more. Fear has departed from them, and intolerable pain, their stomachs did not explode, mud did not slowly drown them nor gas poison them, they died quickly and bravely, not screaming in panic and agony through vomit and blood with their guts hanging out, they are at peace now, Harry and Johnny are at peace, they rest easy in proper graves. Just as I tell myself that Jo sleeps in the forest, under a spread of leaves.

The spirits left me, because I lied. I promised to transmit their messages truthfully yet did not. After 1918 I could no longer work as a medium. I was barren. I'd betrayed my calling and was punished for it. George and Jo were dead and the spirits came to me no more. That was the end of my real life on this earth.

Lily's still so angry about the past, so bitter. At her age. It's true

I never hid from her how much I'd wanted a son, to see George born again in a baby boy, how much I grieved having only a daughter left to me once Jo was killed. I see now it was wrong. But it's too late to mend things with her now. I'm too old and tired. I always loved men more than women. It is hard to love women. They want far too much. They are so prickly, so demanding. I did love Rosina when we were children, but then I tried to stop her becoming a medium, and I took George. So Rosina and I stopped loving each other. I loved my father, then William, then George, then Jo. The men used me up, I hadn't anything left over for women.

I did love Hattie, but she was a spirit, that made her different. And anyway, she had to leave me. I did love my mother, but I was always jealous, she loved my father so much, far more than she loved me. That's exactly what Lily thinks I've done too.

But Lily and I are quite companionable. It would only embarrass her if I started, at my age, telling her I loved her.

Rosie, Rosie, we did once suit each other so well. Before I began to bully you and betray you. Before you punished me. And you're long dead, and I soon shall be.

Today being the day before Christmas Eve, my dear Mamma, I calculate that it is three weeks since I last wrote to you. So much has happened in that time!

I must thank you, first, for the letters you wrote me while I was prostrate upon my sickbed. Their tone of Christian exhortation played no small part, I believe, in my recovery. I am now completely well again, thanks to the rigours of the cure to which I submitted myself. Dr Felton proved himself very much my friend: the severity of his treatments, which I deplored at the time I endured them, has resulted in my regaining, in what he says has been a comparatively short time, in his experience of other lady patients smitten with the sort of nervous collapse that I suffered, all my usual vitality and cheerful willingness to take up my old place in our household. The diet he prescribed for me while I lay abed has resulted in my gaining a great deal of weight: I am grown fat and rosy, my cheeks plumper than they have ever been. I look quite matronly! And I have been forced to have all my waistbands let out. What with attending to my wardrobe, seeing to my babe, and supervising the children's lessons, I have scarcely a moment to call my own. This is all to the good; it prevents too much thinking about the painful events of the past months; it aids me to place things in a correct perspective.

I have been enabled to come to the conclusion that the surges of emotion produced by my attendances at spiritualistic seances were too much for one of my passionate and ardent nature, though at the time they were excitements I was confident that I would not be overwhelmed by. While the seances with Miss Milk initially brought me much comfort and inspiration, their prolonged and repeated occurrence was not, I have now decided, in my best interests. I believe it to be safer for one of my keen sensitivity not to venture onto the shores of occult beliefs and practices; though I remained throughout a faithful Christian, yet was I nearly swept away by the muddy tides of paganism!

Such, you see, is the seductive power of a phenomenon that, though it pretends to be compatible with the strictest adherence to the tenets of the Church, may yet lead the eager seeker after spiritual knowledge into those trackless wastes where he experiences doubt, despair and moral anguish. Many mediums, of course, lead blameless and upright lives, motivated solely by the desire to aid their fellow men; yet I fear that the more susceptible amongst them, in particular perhaps those of the *weaker* sex, are made, by their very openness and availability to the occult forces, potential vessels for Satan! When we consider the phenomenon of possession by spirits in a calm and rational light, it is easy to see how the practice lends itself to abuse if the medium concerned has not, to start with, a fully formed and strongly moral conscience. In the case of *young persons* practising clairaudience and clairvoyance (and many mediums first gain an inkling of their vocations at the tender age of fifteen or sixteen) it is perhaps unsurprising that their undoubted gifts of prophecy and soothsaying may be contaminated by the defects of an immature personality.

Such, at any rate, is William's view. Having observed, in Paris, the deranged young women incarcerated in the wards of the Salpetrière, he has been forced to conclude that all too many young female mediums partake of the moral degeneracy always found amongst hysterics. Their utterances must therefore be treated with the greatest of caution, for, though the severe disturbance of their nervous systems is undeniably compensated for by a high degree of intuition which affords them a seemingly magical sympathy with their auditors, yet, on the other hand, their mental failings render a great deal of their solemnly worded speeches the merest gibberish.

Miss Milk, for example, while in the trance state (a condition which I now see as analogous on occasions to that of medical, emotional and moral collapse) would sometimes turn on me and accuse me not only of having severely neglected poor little Rosalie and so having contributed to her untimely departure from this world but of having similarly neglected my dear husband in order to indulge myself in profligate behaviour with certain of my acquaintances of the male sex! These wild and degenerate rantings were afterwards explained by her as evidence of her occasional possession by bad spirits. While attempting to accept, at the time, her view of the matter, I was nevertheless so distressed by these examples of the dangers of an uncontrolled imagination that I was unable afterwards to treat her with the same degree of consideration and intimacy as before. My faith in my little favourite was severely shaken. And my doubts as to her trustworthiness were corroborated, to no small degree, by Mr Frederick Andrews. He has shown himself to be very much my friend. With the utmost delicacy, the utmost regret at causing me the least distress, he has prevailed upon me to consider seriously the wealth of written evidence now in existence which details the fraud and trickery to which unscrupulous mediums will occasionally stoop in order to increase their status and, I regret to say, their incomes. (He and his sister, I am happy to report, are tireless in their invitations to me to make one of their group again at the seaside this summer.)

William is not at all convinced that Miss Milk was ever party to the sort of deceptions that certain wicked practitioners of that dark art have been proved to stoop to. On the other hand, my dear husband has decided, finally, that the ultimate testing of mediumship rests with the medical doctor and the psychologist rather than with the physicist. He has counselled me, therefore, in the most earnest way, to disregard the wild and fanciful disclosures made by Miss Milk on the subject of our family life, assuring me that to ponder upon them would render *me* susceptible to that same moral contamination. With this advice I instantly and heartily agreed: all my thoughts are now for my living family, my close circle of loved ones. In the mystical realm I no longer take any interest: it is the domestic which commands my attention. Not that dear William has recanted his cautiously positive views of spirit materializations, of course; since he has only recently published his optimistic findings, in *The Spiritualist Magazine*, he can scarcely be expected to go back upon them too soon. Only, he explained to me when I enquired of him upon this topic, he is now willing to concede that these seemingly miraculous events, inexplicable by any thesis so far known to physics, may yet disclose their secrets to the penetration of the nerve specialist. At any rate, he is content to leave to his European brethren the opening up of this dark continent of knowledge, and to return to his former speculations upon electricity. You see, Mamma, the greatness of the man I have married! His modesty, I told him, and his *knowing when to stop*, are exemplary!

One result of this discussion has been our expressed disinclination to invite Miss Milk for another visit. We have done quite enough, I consider, to help her launch herself upon a respectable profession; others may now take that responsibility if they wish; I flatter myself that not all patrons will have that patience with her whimsicalities evinced by William and myself! For there is no denying that a young woman of that unfortunate class and milieu is not a little trying, occasionally, to one's habits of speech and thought. I really had supposed that she had learned enough from me to know that a letter of thanks is generally thought appropriate after a visit of such long duration as hers, but not a word from her did I receive during her sojourn in Essex, nor, she having so hurriedly departed without leaving me her aunt's address, was I able to send her my affectionate enquiries as to how she did. I have therefore written her a note at her mother's assuring her of my continued interest in how she gets on, but my inability, due to the burden of my household duties as Christmas approaches, to receive her here again as a visitor. My tone was perhaps a little hasty; but I could not help it; my warm maternal heart has been disappointed by her ingratitude.

Still, as William so sensibly observed, what else should we expect? Flora was not to be re-educated overnight! Far better, he advised me, to think no more of her, and to put *the whole episode* behind me. Upon my assuring him that I *would*, he became much

moved, praising me for my forbearance and my fortitude.
Indeed, William has made me very happy since his return from
Paris! He sits with me now quite often of an evening, declaring
merrily that his own hearth, pipe and slippers are preferable to
his laboratory and white coat after an arduous day's work, and
he has begun a project on which he long ago set his heart: that of
reading to me all the plays of Shakespeare. So, in the calm and
peace of our family group you may imagine us newly ensconced,
our children around us, and our souls reunited. To my dear
husband, when he is at home, I am now able to open my heart as
of old, and this is a source of no little satisfaction to me. Once
more I may rely upon him for sustenance and advice, once more
I am assured of his complete devotion, once more I am in receipt
of those conjugal caresses it is my wifely *privilege* and *joy*, as well
as my duty, to welcome. My cup of happiness, so newly filled to
the brim, will overflow, I doubt not, when we have the joy of
receiving you here at New Year for your long-deferred visit. Now
I must close. William likes no one else but me, I am sure you
recall, to make tea for him at this hour; I expect him home at any
moment from his club; and I have still got all the children's
presents (to say nothing of their grandmamma's!) to wrap up.
For the moment only therefore, my dearest Mamma, I bid you
adieu.

   Your loving daughter,
     Minny.

*

KING HAT.
HAT KING
HATTIE KING
HATTIE NOT KING
HATTIE NOTHING
HATTIE NOT
HATTIE
HAT
HA
H
O

*

My dear Mr Redburn, I write to you out of the fullness of my heart to thank you, on behalf of both my mother and myself, for our most agreeable stay with you last week. Words cannot express my deep gratitude for all your kindness. Please thank your housekeeper for looking after us so well and seeing that our rooms were made so attractive, your cook for serving us such tempting and appetizing meals, and your gardener who so unselfishly ransacked the hothouses to give us the first of the ripe peaches. We are not used to living like kings! But I suspect we quickly got used to it, and have not ceased, since our return to London, to sing the praises of the good friend who made that possible. I know your modesty, sir, I know you do not like to be thanked too much, so I will not embarrass you with further effusions. Only I would like to tell you, since we are now friends who may speak freely with each other, how much you touched my heart that evening when you told me that you were sure your dear wife would approve of our acquaintance. Believe me, sir, she rests happily on that farther shore, and I am certain that in the course of a future seance we may be able to hear her say so in her own words.

You told me how much, since you have no children, I now stand to you in the light of a daughter. Believe me, sir, I look up to you as *more* than a father, since you have rescued me from doubt and despair by making me so much more confident of my mediumistic gifts. To me you have proved yourself a most precious friend. I stand always in your debt. I am sure I shall be able to repay you, on my next visit, by making contact with your so dear and blessed wife. You will see your loved one again, sir, I am sure of that: now that we have established the materialization of Katy King, we have a good friend in high places!

Without wishing to hurt or offend you, dear Mr Redburn, may I also say that I thank God daily for his astonishing mercy in allowing me to act as the balm to your soul, so grievously wounded by another. How humbly moved I am that, you having suffered so much at the hands of the *one* sister, the *other* should be allowed to heal and restore you! We will not speak of her further. We will not mention her name. Both of us can forgive her now, because she has been the instrument, all unwitting, of God's saving grace. His goodness knows no bounds. He has enabled me to hope that I may be of service to you.

My dear mother sends you her warmest good wishes, and her thanks for all the care with which you so thoughtfully provided us during our stay. You see that I do not quarrel with you, sir, over your insistence on paying for our railway tickets. I do not wish to quarrel with you ever.

I remain your affectionate and sincere friend,
 Rosina Milk.

A Selected List of Titles Available from Minerva

While every effort is made to keep prices low, it is sometimes necessary to increase prices at short notice. Mandarin Paperbacks reserves the right to show new retail prices on covers which may differ from those previously advertised in the text or elsewhere.

The prices shown below were correct at the time of going to press.

Fiction

☐	7493 9026 3	**I Pass Like Night**	Jonathan Ames £3.99	BX
☐	7493 9006 9	**The Tidewater Tales**	John Bath £4.99	BX
☐	7493 9004 2	**A Casual Brutality**	Neil Blessondath £4.50	BX
☐	7493 9028 2	**Interior**	Justin Cartwright £3.99	BC
☐	7493 9002 6	**No Telephone to Heaven**	Michelle Cliff £3.99	BX
☐	7493 9028 X	**Not Not While the Giro**	James Kelman £4.50	BX
☐	7493 9011 5	**Parable of the Blind**	Gert Hofmann £3.99	BC
☐	7493 9010 7	**The Inventor**	Jakov Lind £3.99	BC
☐	7493 9003 4	**Fall of the Imam**	Nawal El Saadewi £3.99	BC

Non-Fiction

☐	7493 9012 3	**Days in the Life**	Jonathon Green £4.99	BC
☐	7493 9019 0	**In Search of J D Salinger**	Ian Hamilton £4.99	BX
☐	7493 9023 9	**Stealing from a Deep Place**	Brian Hall £3.99	BX
☐	7493 9005 0	**The Orton Diaries**	John Lahr £5.99	BC
☐	7493 9014 X	**Nora**	Brenda Maddox £6.99	BC

All these books are available at your bookshop or newsagent, or can be ordered direct from the publisher. Just tick the titles you want and fill in the form below. Available in:
BX: British Commonwealth excluding Canada
BC: British Commonwealth including Canada

Mandarin Paperbacks, Cash Sales Department, PO Box 11, Falmouth, Cornwall TR10 9EN.

Please send cheque or postal order, no currency, for purchase price quoted and allow the following for postage and packing:

UK	80p for the first book, 20p for each additional book ordered to a maximum charge of £2.00.
BFPO	80p for the first book, 20p for each additional book.
Overseas including Eire	£1.50 for the first book, £1.00 for the second and 30p for each additional book thereafter.

NAME (Block letters) ....

ADDRESS ....

....

....